The

Mask

Collector

Andrew Chapman

Copyright © 2022, Andrew Chapman

Andrew Chapman has asserted his right to be identified as the author of this Work in accordance with the Copyright, Designs and Patents Act 1988

All rights reserved. No part of this publication may be reproduced, stored in a retrieval system, or transmitted in any form or by any means, electronic, mechanical, photocopying, recording or otherwise, without the prior permission of the copyright owner

Published by Andrew Chapman,
andrew-chapman@live.co.uk

ALSO BY THIS AUTHOR

Jack's Game

AUTHOR'S NOTE

This book is the product of a single frantic day at the keyboard. I sat down at my desk at 9am on the 12th of May 2022 and I was still there at 9am on the 13th of May (I'm actually writing this with an hour and a half still to go, but I know now that I will make it to 9am and my brain needs a break from the fictional).

I had a goal that I didn't achieve. I thought I could write fifty thousand words in a single sitting (an idea born from *The Bestseller Experiment podcast*). I was wrong. I managed half of that.

I mean, I didn't really think I would be able to do it. I just wanted to try. 50,000 words. It's an absurd number. It's short for a novel, which average around 70,000, but the average novel takes a year to write. I was trying to do it in a day.

I both failed and succeeded. I told the whole story. It was complete when I finished. It was just much shorter than I had hoped. I ran out of road.

If I were to attempt it again (very unlikely—though it wasn't an unpleasant experience), I would probably not adapt a screenplay. I thought doing that was a clever trick to save on having to think about what happens next.

I wrote the screenplay of *The Mask Collector* during the first Covid lockdown. A complete feature-length film. And a good one too. In the words of Mark Stay, it had blockbuster potential.

When the idea came to attempt this feat, adapting it seemed like the obvious thing to do. A screenplay is basically a very detailed outline. The problem is, it's too detailed. I was caged in. I couldn't let go and fly. It was a machine job of mechanically re-describing scenes that already existed with little scope for improvement, as it had already been worked and reworked in its original format.

If I had come up with a completely new idea and given myself a far looser outline, I might have been able to get in the zone and lose myself in rapid fire prose.

But I'll be honest. The goal of reaching a big word count is a shallow one. Story is king. That's the most important thing. Authors often forget that. We get carried away with what is expected and don't let the story tell itself at its own pace. I didn't succeed in writing a novel, but I did succeed in writing a novella. A lot of my favourite books are novellas (*The Great Gatsby, Animal Farm, The Metamorphosis, The Heart of Darkness, The Strange Case of Dr Jekyll and Mr Hyde, The Body, Rita Hayworth and Shawshank Redemption, The Langoliers, The Mist, The Rats, The Hellbound Heart, War of the Worlds*—should I go on?) and I've been writing a lot of them recently.

Under the penname, Elwood Flynn, I've been intentionally

writing thirty-five-thousand-word pulp westerns. I love reading them and I love writing them. I like the leanness of the prose. The challenge of pairing the language back to its most raw form. It's no wonder this ended short.

One of the great things that came from this was that I got to rediscover *The Mask Collector* as a reader. I had forgotten a lot of the script. I hadn't realised how much of it I had forgotten until I started this experiment. It surprised me. What surprised me more was how entertained I was. I felt the suspense of the intended viewer/reader as I adapted it. I fell in love with the characters all over again.

A lot of the people reading this were there with me the day I wrote this. So many fellow authors and readers rallied around me and tweeted all day and night cheering me on and offering support (you got it to number ten in the horror charts between Stephen King and Stephen King, and it hadn't even been written yet). It was a great day. An excellent way to spend a birthday. I was doing what I loved with the people that I love. The teenager was at her mother's studying for her GCSEs, which start next week, but Rachel and the cat were here, cracking the whip (and making me coffee).

When things got desperate, at about 3am when the story was done and I didn't know what to do to make the book fatter, I had a radical idea. The main character in the book is Pat Caine. He is a famous retired bank robber who wrote a very successful book about his life of crime. That was it! I could write chapters from his book, from his point of view, and place them randomly throughout the book! Problem solved.

I wrote two chapters. Told two stories from his early life. In one, Caine is fourteen and getting up to some thieving hijinks involving a milk float. In the other, he is twenty-four and planning his first bank robbery.

When it came to placing them in the story, all it did was slow down the pace. They were jarring. I have included them at the end of the main story for your amusement. They were written by an exhausted mind at an ungodly hour.

So, without further ado, I present to you, *The Mask Collector*. It was written with passion and sleep deprivation. I think it shows. I hope you enjoy it. Be kind with your reviews.

I think you will like DCI Conrad. I'm sorry there's not more of her. Another book maybe. Another time.

Andrew Chapman – 7:45am, 13th of May 2022, Bournemouth.

*For Vin, Rachel, Calcifer,
and everyone in the BXP community.
You are all beautiful, wonderful creatures.*

'And now, the main event. So, turn off your phones, finish your conversations, and get ready. It's about to begin.'

- ODEON cinema

CHAPTER ONE

BAILEY Towers was a block of flats that had been ignored by the council, forgotten by God, and destroyed by its occupants. It was a grey spray-painted monolith of bored souls and empty beer cans.

Pat Caine lived on the sixth floor.

He closed the door to his flat, calling in to his wife as he did. 'I'm just popping out for an hour.'

He didn't wait for a reply. Pat was a man in his seventies. Tall and fit. Wearing a long black coat and a flat cap.

Leaning against the banister was a man dressed identically. His name was Grey. Told people he was from the Cayman Islands, but Caine knew that was a load of old bollocks. He was born in Hackney. He was a big black guy and Caine's oldest friend.

'Pat Caine,' said Grey.

'You ready for this?' said Pat, starting towards the lift.

'It's broken.'

Caine sighed. 'Stairs then.'

They headed down shoulder to shoulder. Caine stepped over a hypodermic needle halfway down to the fifth floor and shook his head as he passed it. 'I'll be glad to see the back of this fucking place.'

'It's not so bad here, the people are nice.'

'The people who live in these flats are criminals.'

'We are criminals, Pat.'

'But we are good criminals. These are stupid criminals. And there is a difference. Anyone can stick a guy with a knife and nick his phone. And what good does it do? Some innocent guy gets hurt, or possibly killed, and our weed-hungry tweaker gets four quid of credit, some stranger's dick pics, and last year's iPhone, which probably has a cracked screen. What's the point in that? No, what we do is different. Very different.'

Rapid footsteps echoed up from below, getting louder. A kid, eleven, came running up the stairs and stopped when he saw Caine and Grey, a look of recognition in his eyes. Looked like a school kid caught skiving. Which he was.

'Alright, Pat. Grey.'

Caine looked the boy up and down while Grey engaged him in small talk.

'You coming to the barbecue on the green this weekend?'

'Yeah, I think so.'

'You got a graffiti can behind your back today?' said Caine.

The kid showed his hands. 'We're not doing that anymore. Like you said.' He looked at Grey. 'We're a community.'

'That's right, good lad.'

Grey smiled and there was real kindness in his eyes. Caine, on the other hand, looked like a head teacher annoyed at a kid for pissing on his shoes.

'Alright, clear off,' said Caine.

The kid shouldered between the two men and took off up the stairs. They listened to him bound up the next flight, and then up again.

'You see,' said Grey, 'That's the effect of my barbecues bringing the community together. I told you it would help this place. It's harder to steal from the old woman next door when you've played with her dog on the green.'

'Or, he's a lying piece of shit.'

'Or, he's a lying piece of shit.' Grey agreed.

Out on the green, down the bottom of the path that ran between the entrance to Bailey Towers and the road, was another person dressed in a long black coat and flat cap.

His name was Sticky, and he was what you might call a delinquent local youth. He lived in the flats too and couldn't be trusted to even hold a door open for you without stealing the door handle.

Behind him, on the road, was a beat-up old Transit van.

'Well, aren't you a handsome couple,' said Sticky, grinning.

'Everything ready, Sticky?' said Caine.

'Yeah, everyone's 'ere.'

Caine nodded. 'Good, get in the van.'

Sticky doffed his cap and did as he was told. Caine and Grey shared a look.

'Fucking bell-end,' said Caine. 'Grey, you get in the back as well. I'll get in the front with Charlie.'

Grey nodded and followed the kid.

In the driver's seat was Charlie. He had a running cheetah with its tail on fire tattooed on his forearm and tyre tracks tattooed around his neck. He had the word MOVE tattooed on the knuckles of his right hand and FAST on his left.

Caine sat next to him. The van shook as Grey got in the back and slammed the doors shut.

'Alright, Charlie?' said Caine.

Charlie gave a single nod.

Caine looked over his shoulder. 'Everyone in?'

There were four people in the back. Grey and Sticky, who we've already met, and Danny and Mills.

Two wooden benches ran along each side of the van. Opposite each other at the back were Sticky and Grey. Next to Grey was Mills and opposite him was Danny, both wearing the same long black coats.

On the floor between them was a duffle bag.

Mills—mid-forties, shoulder length hair, bit of a left-wing revolutionist in his youth—was reading that day's *Morning Star* newspaper, which he raised in salute to Caine. 'We're all here. Let's go fuck the man, shall we?'

'We're not here to fuck any men, Mills, but yes, let's get a move on. You alright there, Danny?'

Danny—long beard, side-parted short hair; looked like the stylised hipster silhouette you see in every barber shop window these days, and wearing leather harness boots and a shirt and waistcoat under his black coat—was reading a comic (the latest issue of *The Department of Truth*). He generally had little interest in basic communication. He didn't answer.

'He's reading his comic,' said Mills.

'I can see that. We got everything?'

'Just as we planned,' said Mills.

'Good,' said Caine. 'Charlie, you know the way.'

Caine's gang. Probably the shittest gang ever put together for the goal of robbing a bank. They wouldn't cope in a high-concept all-brains-swinging heist job. Ocean's Eleven they were not. But for what Caine had planned, they'd do.

CHAPTER TWO

CHARLIE started the engine and gunned the accelerator. The wheels spun, filling the green with the choking smell of burnt rubber. The van lurched into the road. Charlie put his foot down, leaned back in his seat, arms straight, hands gripped on the wheel, like he was about to go back in time in a DeLorean.

Caine swore. Shunted left into the door.

Charlie changed up a gear. Wheels on either side of the centre line.

'Not so fast, Charlie. You stick to the traffic laws on the way there and drive like a cunt on the way back. We're not going to get pulled over before we even start.'

Charlie swerved past a cyclist, causing an old woman in a fifteen-year-old Nissan Micra to bump up onto the pavement on the other side to avoid him. Charlie hit the clutch and went up to third. The engine was howling.

'He doesn't know how to drive slow,' said Mills.

Caine opened his jacket, showing the curved handle of a six-shot revolver.

'If we get pulled over, I'll shoot you where you sit.'

Charlie glanced over. Rolled his eyes. Slowed down. Caine

closed his coat.

'Right. Good.' Caine looked back at Mills, who was grinning from between the headrests. 'Sit down, Mills.' Mills retreated. 'Now, we've got about ten minutes' drive before we get there so get yourselves into the right mind-set. It will be quick. In and out. No fuckin' around.'

The van indicated left and rounded a corner.

The four men were laughing and joking in the back.

Caine opened the glove box and rummaged inside. Found a CD case. Read the cover and looked at Charlie.

'Classical Masterpieces?' Charlie glanced at the CD and shrugged. 'Got nothing better?'

'I can sing if you want?'

'What's on the radio?'

'It's stuck on Radio 4.' He looked at the time on the dashboard. 'I think it's Woman's Hour.'

Caine contemplated slapping him. Put the CD in the car stereo. It spun and whirred. Vivaldi's *Concerto for violin in G Minor* began to play.

Sticky turned to Grey in the back.

'What did you bring?'

Grey smiled. Opened his coat. Two handles with brown leather grips protruded from both inside pockets.

'Knives?'

'Machetes.'

'Nice.'

'What about you?'

Sticky took a hammer from his left pocket and a flick-knife from the right.

'You can't go wrong with that. What about you, Mills?'

Mills had a newspaper open and was shaking his head at what he was reading.

'A samurai sword. Have you seen this shit?'

Danny looked up from his comic. Glanced at the front page. Returned to his comic.

The headline read; THE MASK COLLECTOR STRIKES AGAIN. The whole front page was taken up by the photo of a young Japanese tourist. London Bridge. Selfie. Big smile. Kind eyes. Looked like a good guy. There were smaller pictures around the photo of the tourist. Sixteen of them. All victims. Different ages, sexes, nationalities. It was a pick 'n' mix of death.

Mills was looking at the two-page spread inside. A covered body on the banks of the Thames. A female detective looking down at it. DCI Conrad. A defeated look on her face.

'A samurai sword? Where the fuck did you get a samurai sword?' said Grey.

Mills looked up from his paper. Saw Sticky and Grey's blank faces.

'Market. It was either that or the sword from ThunderCats.'

'Sword of Omens. Eye of Thundera,' said Danny, quietly, not looking away from his comic.

They all looked at him and then back at Mills, who reached

behind his back and unsheathed the sword.

'You know those swords at the market are just for display, right? They're blunt,' said Sticky.

'I know. I took it home and sharpened it.'

Danny finished his comic and put it on the bench beside him.

'What did you bring?' said Grey.

'Axe,' said Danny, but didn't show it. He looked out over the headrests at the passing high street. Sighed like the world was pressing down on him.

'Okay,' said Sticky, looking at the others with an expression on his face that very clearly read, *He is fucking nuts.*

Mills picked the newspaper back up.

'They found another body.'

'It's fucking sick, mate,' Sticky leaned forward, 'Do you know why they call him The Mask Collector?'

'Because the bodies are found with their skulls de-gloved,' said Grey.

'Apparently he's got a basement full of those mannequin heads with all the faces of those people he killed on 'em and he dances around with 'em on. To like, Korean pop music or something.'

'Korean pop music?' said Grey.

'That's what I heard. Fucking sick, mate.'

'Where do you get this shit?'

'It's just what people are sayin'.'

The van pulled up at a curb and stopped. Charlie killed the

ignition and the music died with it.

Caine turned in his seat to face his crew.

'Alright, this is it. Now, I know you all know this but we're going to go through it once more. We keep things simple. This sort of thing doesn't go down like it does in the movies, and I would know. There's no complicated plot. We go in, wave a gun around.' He held up his scuffed old six-shooter revolver. 'You lot act scary and keep everyone away from their phones and those sneaky little silent alarm buttons under their desks, and then we take all the money. No fucking around. In and out. Got it? Good. Now, put on your balaclavas, make sure your weapons are nice and shiny, and follow me. Charlie, you stay here. We'll be back in a tick.'

CHAPTER THREE

There were four cashier windows in the bank. All busy.

A teenage boy left one of the windows and headed for the door. The cashier—green necktie and green pinstriped waistcoat—called the next in line.

It was a big bank. High ceiling and oak counters. Old stone walls. Constructed when banks were built like churches.

To the left of the cashier windows were the private rooms for mortgage and loans advice. To the right of the cashier windows was a customer service desk. It was the only counter in the main lobby not protected by bulletproof glass. Out in the open.

A female member of staff, with the name Catherine on her badge, was helping a thin man, who was leaning casually against the counter while she typed his name into the computer: Nick Priest.

The teenager reached for the handle, just as the door burst open. Everyone flinched and looked up from what they were doing. The kid stumbled backwards and fell over.

Caine entered, pulled his gun, and cocked the hammer.

The rest of the gang came in around him.

Caine stepped over the teenager, and Mills closed the door, ramming the bolts home.

Sticky dropped the duffle bag and sprang his flick knife. Grey drew his machetes. Danny stood casually, axe at his side.

Caine coughed.

'Good afternoon, everybody. This is a robbery. We're going to keep this simple. If no one wants to die all you have to do is follow three simple instructions.'

Caine held up a finger.

'One, get the fuck away from your desks and put your hands in the air.'

A second finger joined the first.

'Two, if you are on this side of the cashier windows you will let my friends here escort you to the corner of the room, where you will remain obedient until this thing is over. One of my colleagues will be collecting your phones but you can have them back once the show is over.'

Caine extended his thumb to complete the trio.

'Three, if you are on the other side of the windows you will stand in the middle of that area, away from any alarms or phones. We will be with you in just a moment. If you decide to be a hero and reach for your phone or the alarm, one of these fine gentlemen will start hacking away at your customers. Got it? Good.'

The cashiers stepped away from their windows and moved to the centre of the back area with their hands up.

Grey, Sticky, and Danny herded the customers into the corner between the cashier windows and the private offices.

'Give me your phones,' said Sticky, holding the duffle bag open.

They hesitated for a moment. Eyes wide with fear. Grey stepped forward and turned the blade of his machete, so it caught the light. It was motivating. The customers obliged and started hurriedly filling the bag with all sorts. Phones, house keys, balled up tissue, loose pennies.

Nick Priest stayed put at the counter. Watching with detached interest.

'You forgot one,' said Caine.

Danny walked over and stood in front of Priest, expecting him to get the message and join the others in the corner.

Priest didn't move.

Danny grabbed him by the arm and pulled him hard, catching him off balance. He threw him in the direction of the others. Priest stumbled sideways and hit the cashier counter hard on his side, hurting his ribs.

His face flushed red, and he stood, half crouched with his right arm holding the pain in his ribs. He stared at Danny. A primal anger in his eyes.

Grey stepped between Danny and Priest with his two machetes at his side.

Priest walked backwards slowly, still crouched, and sat with the other hostages. He never took his eyes off Danny.

Caine turned his attention back to the girl behind the desk.

'Right. Now, step back from the desk and open the door.'

He motioned to the door that led to the back area with his gun and then aimed it at her.

She didn't move.

'Are you deaf?'

She started to lower her hand. Keeping her eyes steady on his.

'Don't you fucking dare.'

She paused and then lowered her hand some more.

Caine held his gun firmer, his arm straight. 'If you press that button, I will shoot you.'

She stopped for a moment. Her eyes remained fixed on his. Calling his bluff. She lowered her hand some more.

Caine took an agitated step forward. 'I will fucking kill you. Don't test me.'

'You're Pat Caine, right?'

Caine didn't reply. The gang shared a concerned look.

Her hand reached under the desk. She paused.

'Don't press that fucking button. I will fucking shoot you. Do you really want to die just so you can be a hero? I'm going to rob this bank whether you're dead or alive.'

His finger tensed on the trigger.

She pressed the button.

'You fucking bitch.'

He tensed his arm, his knuckles turning white as he gripped the gun harder. Anger on his face. He squeezed the trigger to the halfway point and the hammer started to pull back.

CHAPTER FOUR

CAINE aimed at her forehead. His arm started to shake.

He wasn't going to pull that trigger. The whole game would be up in an instant if he did. He lowered the gun.

Catherine smiled.

'Fuck,' said Caine.

A sense of cocky confidence prevailed among the staff who were safely behind the counter. One of them, a thin man named Dominic, took his phone out of his pocket. He dialled a three-digit number and put the phone to his ear.

Caine saw him and aimed the gun at the cashier window. It was no secret the glass was bulletproof. Caine knew it. Dominic knew it.

'Put your phone away,' said Caine.

Dominic smirked and raised a cocky eyebrow. He had short dark hair. Reminded Caine of Pee-wee Herman, only rounder in the face. 'Bulletproof glass, mate. Hello? Yes, police please.'

Danny, having grown bored of this spectacle, stepped around Caine and walked to the back of the customer service desk. Catherine backed away from him. More afraid of Danny than she was of Caine, but still cocky.

No telling what was going on in Danny's mind. The best psychiatrists in the world couldn't tell you. Best guess: there are no thoughts. It's just noise. Like the thickest string on a bass guitar reverberating around his skull with no let up. He was always distracted but always knew what was going on and the quickest way to solve a problem. He was all the way focused and all the way distracted, all the time. Scared the shit out of most people just by being near them.

Danny started to raise his axe.

'Danny,' said Caine, a warning.

Danny looked at Caine and then back at Catherine. He considered his options and came to a conclusion.

He put his axe down.

She smiled.

Danny grabbed her by the wrist, slammed her hand down on the desk, picked up the chained pen, and stabbed it through the back of her hand.

The sound of it sticking into the wood reverberated around the bank like a firm KNOCK.

Her hand was pinned down. She stared for a weird moment and then screamed. Dominic joined her. It was a scream like Tippi Hedren in Alfred Hitchcock's *The Birds*. It was satisfying, in a way. A good old-fashioned scream. You don't get to hear those too often these days. It felt nostalgic. If you were into that sort of thing.

'Told you he was mental,' said Sticky.

Danny stepped away and walked back around the desk to

Caine's side.

Caine looked at him. Danny nodded in a way that said, *sorted that problem out.*

Caine looked at Catherine. Tears were running down her cheeks. She tried to pull the pen out without causing more pain. Couldn't do it. She let go of the pen. Held her pinned arm by the wrist. Started to breathe like a panic attack was on its way.

'What's the code for the door?' said Caine.

Dominic suddenly looked very afraid. He threw his phone away and put his hands back in the air.

'Two-seven-one-two,' said Catherine.

'That wasn't so hard, was it?'

Caine's ear turned to the main door. The faint sound of sirens could be heard coming towards the bank.

Caine headed to the door behind Catherine and pressed the code into the number pad. A light turned green, and the door clicked open. He turned back to Catherine.

'This could have been so easy. No one had to get hurt. In and out. Insurance covers your loss, and we disappear. But you decided to be brave. And now look what we have. A hostage situation.'

Catherine spoke through the pain. 'It is you, isn't it? Pat Caine?'

Their eyes locked.

'Right? That's why you didn't shoot me.'

Caine didn't respond.

While the gang was distracted by the back and forth

between Catherine and Caine, Nick Priest peeled away from the other customers and quietly moved to the opposite corner of the foyer. He got down behind a freestanding banner advertising security assured banking.

'Come on, I recognise your voice. Famous ex-bank robber. Served your time. Wrote that book, what was it? *The Threat of Violence*? About how you pride yourself on victimless crime. You never hurt anyone. I guess that was a lie. You're just a thug.'

Pissed off, Caine pulled his balaclava off. Stormed up to her and pointed a finger at the pen sticking out of her hand.

'This is on you. All you had to do is what you were told. But you had to stoke the fire. You got burnt. That's your fault, not mine.'

Caine put the code in the door again and held it open.

Sticky pulled his balaclava off.

'What are you doing?' said Grey.

'Taking my balaclava off. Caine took his off.'

'But nobody knew who you were.'

Mills took his off. 'I think the cat is out of the bag, Grey. Cops are already outside.'

'Yeah, say my name. That's fine. Cheers mate.'

Grey took his balaclava off and chucked it aside.

They looked at Danny. He was reading a pamphlet about pensions. Noticed he was being watched and looked at the others. He took his balaclava off, folded it up, and put it in his coat pocket, then returned to the pamphlet.

'Could you maybe start bringing the hostages through?'

said Caine.

Grey and Sticky forced the hostages to their feet and ushered them into the back room.

Mills approached Catherine with his hands out in a friendly gesture. She was on her knees, trying to keep her hand still on the counter.

'What's your name?'

'Catherine.'

'Catherine, I'm going to pull the pen out.'

She closed her eyes tight and bowed her head. Nodded.

Mills gripped the pen. It moved a bit and blood rose out of the wound.

'Ow, fuck! Just pull it out,' she said.

Mills pulled. It came out with a wet pop.

Her hand slid off the desk and she cradled it in her other. Mills helped her up. Walked her round back.

'Danny, check those rooms for more hostages,' said Caine.

Danny looked at the private offices and nodded. He walked across the foyer, axe in hand, and entered.

Caine turned away and started helping the others with the hostages.

Nick Priest stepped out from behind his hiding place and slipped into the private office as the door was still closing behind Danny.

CHAPTER FIVE

Caine made a gap in the blinds and looked out at the road. He was in a side office in the back area. Two police cars drove past, lights flashing, and stopped, joining three police vehicles that were already parked outside.

He moved away from the window and left the office.

Sticky and Grey were tying the hostage's hands behind their backs and taping their mouths.

The bank uniform, male or female, had ties. Green, to match their waistcoats. They put the ties between their teeth and tied them at the back. Then applied the gaffer tape.

Grey had grown up with Caine. They shared an outlook. Both despised violence. They were not morons; they knew that what they did was not innocent or noble. They were guilty of glorifying the deed in their minds, and in stories down the pub (and literally in the case of Caine's infamous autobiography), but they knew it was wrong. They made it okay by making sure, as much as they could, that nobody got hurt. Maybe it was a bit beyond them to consider mental damage and trauma, but pain and physical violence? That was not in their wheelhouse.

Grey pressed the tape to a young girl's lips and thought of the old days, when it was just him and Caine. Still, you gotta do what you gotta do.

Mills was bandaging Catherine's hand. He was being overly tender. Kept trying to catch her eye as he did it. Like this was the perfect situation to spark a romance.

Caine looked at her wound and then out at the main foyer, visible through the cashier windows.

'Where is Danny?' he said.

'He went to check that room out,' said Grey.

'He's taking his fucking time.'

As he said it, the door to the office opened and Danny stepped out.

Caine saw him. 'Finally. Get back here and help this lot tie up the hostages.'

He turned away from Danny and opened the door. He pulled a chair in front of it to keep it open.

When he turned back, he saw that Danny had stopped.

He was standing there. Still and rigid. Staring through the cashier windows at them.

'What are you—' Caine stopped. He struggled to register what he was seeing.

The eyes of the hostages, with their mouths taped shut, widened with fear. All of them staring at Danny. They started to panic and scream under the tape.

Mills, Grey, and Sticky, all stopped what they were doing and looked at Danny.

At first, they frowned. Could see something was wrong but

couldn't figure out what. Then they saw it.

Danny's face was slightly wonky.

Inside his mouth was a second pair of lips. His eyelids were stretched awkwardly, and a second pair of eyelids were visible inside them. Cold steady eyes looked out of them. Eyes that were not Danny's eyes.

There was a split up the back of Danny's head and the skin, with his dark hair, was curled apart revealing mousy blond hair beneath.

Nick Priest was wearing Danny's skin, a full head mask. He was also wearing his coat, and his waistcoat under it.

He moved towards the door.

Caine stood stunned, watched, too shocked to move.

Sticky dropped his roll of tape and ran past Caine. He kicked the chair out of the way and slammed the door shut.

The moment it closed, the handle slammed down. The door didn't budge.

Sticky stepped cautiously away. Everybody in the back area watched.

There were four beeps. Slow. Considered. Each number chosen carefully. There was a harsh buzz notifying that the code was wrong.

Sticky turned to Caine. 'It's the fucking Mask Collector.'

Four more beeps. Slow. Considered. A different tone. The correct code. The door handle went down, and the door clicked open.

CHAPTER SIX

CHARLIE fidgeted in the van. Listening to Radio 4. It was the intro to *The Archers*. He liked Radio 4. Didn't used to. Was a Radio 1 guy. Never really grew out of it. Used to like listening to Chris Moyles in the morning when he was a teenager, while out joyriding in other people's cars.

It was only since he'd pinched this van a few months ago that he'd started listening to Radio 4, because of the broken stereo. He found it calming. Found it easier to drift around corners with Mariella Frostrup talking about books in her deeply sexy voice. It centred him. Figured maybe he was starting to get cultured. Even bought a classical CD to listen to. He bought a book as well. It was called *Ulysses*. He couldn't read it. It was an unreadable pile of shit, but the thought was there.

He watched the scene outside the bank get busier with cops and curious pedestrians and shook his head. Tutted.

He had his phone in his hands with WhatsApp open. The last message read, 'It's on.'

The reply from Charlie was a cartoon GIF of a burglar with a swag bag.

Charlie wrote a new message, 'Everything OK?' and pressed send.

He put his phone away. *The Archers* theme had only been playing for the trailer. Too early in the day for that. And thank fuck. He had no interest in cows.

A sort of documentary show came on about stolen Gods in Cambodia. They wanted their statues back. It was interesting. He'd learned a lot since he started listening to Radio 4.

He leaned back in his seat behind the steering wheel, the place he felt most at home, and watched the show unfold outside.

An unmarked police car drove past Charlie's van and found a space to pull into among the rest of the police cars.

The engine stopped. The door opened. A man stepped out.

Older guy. Wise face. Grey hair. Jeans and shirt. Looked more like a science lecturer than a police officer. His name was Iain O'Neil.

'You the guy?' said a female police officer.

'I think I might be. What's the situation?'

'We don't know yet. The alarms have sounded, and the doors have been locked from the inside. We've had no contact so far. Just a call to nine-nine-nine about a robbery in progress.'

O'Neil nodded and looked around. It was noisy. People were gathered on the street, staring. Reporters were starting to show up. A young mum with a pram was complaining loudly about the bank being shut. He spotted a café opposite the bank.

'I'll be in there. Get me the number for the bank.'

'You're going for a coffee? Now?'

He didn't answer.

The policewoman watched O'Neil walk away and head into the café.

O'Neil said something to the customers, and they filed out of the café. He locked the door behind them and then said something to the barista behind the counter. He took a window seat and retrieved a notepad from his bag, put it on the table, and took a pencil from his shirt pocket.

The barista brought him a coffee.

'Who was that?' said a policeman.

'The negotiator,' said the policewoman.

'What's he doing in a café?'

'I don't know. You got the number for the bank?'

'Yeah, here.'

'Give it to him.'

The policeman walked across the road to the café door and tried to open it. O'Neil beckoned with a finger. The policeman went to the window.

'I've got the number for the bank.'

O'Neil tapped on the window.

'What? You want me to hold the number up to the window?'

O'Neil waited. The policeman unfolded a piece of paper and pressed it against the window.

O'Neil copied down the number at the top of his notepad. He didn't look back up at the policeman, who got the hint and left.

CHAPTER SEVEN

CAINE and Sticky put all their weight against the door but struggled against the surprising strength of Nick Priest on the other side. They leaned into it and the door just kept coming. It was like a magnet fighting against the opposing force of another.

Grey ran up and put his full body into it and the door slammed shut.

'Mills, get the lock,' said Grey.

Mills pushed the bolt into the slot at the top of the door.

They all stepped back. The handle jerked a few times. There was a pause. The code went. Four beeps followed by a sound that indicated that the code was correct. The handle went again. The door stayed shut.

They watched as The Mask Collector walked back through the main foyer.

Nick stopped and stared at them for a moment and then looked around, considering his next move. Walked calmly to the private office and entered. The door closed gently behind him.

'What are we going to do, Pat?' said Grey.

Dominic managed to get the tie loose by moving his head around and he spat it free from his mouth. They hadn't got around to gaffer taping his gob shut yet.

'You could tell the police there is a serial killer in here with us and hand yourselves in so none of us have to die.'

'No. That is not what we're going to do. I'm not going back to prison because some cunt likes wearing people's faces. That's got nothing to do with me. Somebody re-gag him. And make sure it's tight this time,' said Caine.

Mills raised the tie and pulled it between Dominic's teeth and made a tight knot at the back of his neck.

The dial inside Sticky's brain that controlled anxiety had been turned up to eleven and his body was showing it. Pacing. Wild hand gestures. Manic expression. 'Mate, this has gone to shit. What are we supposed to do? Finish robbing the bank? How the fuck are we going to do that? Danny is dead, mate.'

Caine put a hand on his shoulder. 'Sticky, you're my nephew, and I love you. But don't call me mate. I have no intentions of ever mating with you, or any other bloke, thank you very much.'

Grey stepped forward. 'Caine, our faces are all over the CCTV. We're surrounded by police. We're trapped in here with a psycho, and I'm meant to be having a barbecue on Saturday. All our plans are up the shitter, and none of us are getting out of here with any amount of money. We'll be lucky to get out with the skin still on our skulls.'

'You're not afraid of that little prick, are you? He took Danny by surprise. He doesn't have that advantage over the rest of us.'

'I could quite happily just walk out that door and let the police do what they want with me. Danny's dead. I mean, come on. He's fucking dead, Caine,' said Mills.

'Why do people keep telling me Danny's dead? Do you think I'm blind? What I need right now is time to think. We are going to get out of this. We are going to get our money, get out of that shithole we call home, and no one else is going to get hurt.'

A phone on the desk started to ring.

'Could be the cops,' said Grey.

'Or it could be some old bird calling about her pension.'

Caine picked up the phone but didn't say anything.

In the café, O'Neil had his phone to his ear and a pencil in his hand. He knew someone was on the line but he said nothing.

Caine could hear O'Neil breathing. The phone clicked off and the line went dead. Caine put the phone down.

'Well, he was chatty.'

The phone rang again. Caine picked it up.

'What?' he said.

'Hello, who am I speaking to?'

'You can call me Captain Cunt. What can I call you?'

'My name is Iain O'Neil.'

'What are you, a cop? Reporter?'

'I'm the lead crisis negotiator. I work closely with the Special Firearms Command, who are currently parked outside. Are you armed, Captain Cunt?'

'As a matter of fact, I am. You're actually going with Captain Cunt?'

'That's the name you gave me. You want me to call you something else?'

'You don't have to call me anything. All you have to do is listen.'

'You have my full attention.'

'We have a handful of hostages and a couple of bags that will soon be full of money. No one has to get hurt and the money is insured. If you want this to end peacefully all you have to do is help facilitate our unhindered departure. Got it?'

'I recognise your voice. Have we spoken before?'

'Maybe you've seen me on telly.'

'Are you an actor?'

'I host morning television. You have the privilege of negotiating with Philip Schofield. I got bored of interviewing lunatics and have turned to a life of crime.'

'A bank robber with a sense of humour?' There was silence for a moment. 'How about this. As a show of faith, why don't you let one of the hostages go and I'll start arranging your arrest-free getaway.'

'Just like that?'

'Just like that.'

'O'Neil, I would love to take you up on your offer. Call me back in ten minutes, would you? I need to confer with my colleagues.'

'I'll be happy to stay on the line and wait.'

The line went dead. O'Neil looked at his blank notepad and thought while tapping his pencil on the pad. Then he wrote the words, *Pat Caine?*

CHAPTER EIGHT

Caine turned away from the phone and addressed the room.

'Well, he can't be trusted. The robbery goes on as normal. Sticky, unpack the bags. Mills, start filling them with cash from the tills. Me and Grey will go down to the safe. Where's the manager?'

Dominic reluctantly put his hand up.

'You?'

He nodded and smiled apologetically under his gag and put his hand back down.

Sticky opened the duffle bag. Inside were more duffle bags, folded away. He took them out and put them on the floor. Grey picked two of them up.

'What about The Mask Collector?' said Catherine.

'Keep an eye out for him,' said Caine.

Mills put a comforting hand on her bandaged one. Trying to be charming. She winced at the pain.

'I think we're safe back here,' he said.

Grey removed the tape from Dominic's mouth with one quick and unexpected pull and pulled the tie loose again. He yelled at the brief but stinging pain.

He rubbed his lips and led the men down the back stairwell to the safe.

Caine and Grey carried a duffle bag each.

They reached a door at the bottom. It was locked. A number pad at the side. Dominic punched in a four-digit code. It was the same code as upstairs. Predictably lax security, as Caine had become used to in his days. It beeped and the door opened.

They entered the safe room, leaving the door ajar behind them.

Ahead was an ornate floor-to-ceiling circular safe. The anteroom to the safe was cluttered with crap. An ad-hoc storage cupboard. There were boxes of leaflets and withdrawal forms stacked along one side.

A smaller safe stood on the floor to the right with two wooden chairs next to it. A packet of cards and two mugs that hadn't been cleared away from a breaktime game of gin.

'Just need to get the keys,' said Dominic.

He knelt in front of the safe and started turning the dial.

'You keep the keys for the safe in a safe?' said Caine.

'Where else am I supposed to keep them?'

'Fair point.'

In the main foyer, the door to the private office opened. Nick Priest came out backwards, carrying a metal watercooler that had been plumbed in and fixed to the wall in the office.

Water was dripping out of the pipes and bits of wallpaper and plasterboard were still hanging on.

Sticky and Mills were taking money out of the tills and filling their duffle bags when they saw him.

They stopped and watched as Priest, still wearing Danny's face, carried the watercooler into the middle of the foyer and turned towards them.

He stepped back and took a running throw. Launched the watercooler at the middle cashier window.

Mills and Sticky ducked instinctively and stepped back.

The watercooler dented on impact and a spiderweb of cracks danced across the glass.

The watercooler crashed to the ground and a puddle of water leaked out.

Mills and Sticky spat curses simultaneously. A 'Fuck' from Mills, and 'Holy shit' from Sticky.

They looked up from their stances. Arms protective over their heads. Saw the glass hadn't smashed. They watched Priest.

Dejected, Priest went back into the office.

'Do you think he can break through?' said Sticky.

'Nah, if it's bulletproof, it's definitely watercooler proof.'

The office door opened again, and Priest emerged holding Danny's axe. He motioned to it and then did a 'Duh' gesture, slapping himself on his the forehead.

He marched forwards and swung back and hit the window hard. The axe head stuck in the glass.

Mills and Sticky took another step back, suddenly uncertain about the relative safety of the glass. Bullets? Sure. But psychopaths with axes? They would have to refer to the manufacturer's specs for that one.

Priest pulled the axe free and swung again, and again, and again.

Mills and Sticky turned away from him and looked at the scared faces of the hostages.

They were all urging Mills and Sticky to do something. Gesturing with their heads.

They looked down at the sword in Mills' hand. The hostages nodded more enthusiastically.

Sticky looked at Mills. 'You're the one with the sword, mate.'

'Right, yeah. But it's Danny.'

'That's not Danny. It's just a fucking psycho wearing his face.'

'Oh yeah, that's much better.'

Priest hit the glass again and it came loose from the frame and smashed to the ground. The Mask Collector started to climb through.

Mills took his samurai sword from its sheath and held it above his head. His legs were trembling.

He swung down hard and struck Priest on the shoulder, cutting him, but not deeply.

He swung again. Priest twisted out of the way and the blade hit the counter with a sharp PANG. The sword snapped at the handle and the blade clattered to the floor.

'Told you that sword was a pile of shit,' said Sticky.

'Danny thought it was cool.'

'Danny was a nutcase.'

'He wasn't. He was just misunderstood. What are you waiting for? Hit him with your hammer.'

Sticky looked back at the bank of desks. His hammer was next to the phone.

'No time,' said Sticky.

'So hit him with your fists.'

Sticky cocked a fist and Priest looked up at him. He was halfway through the tight window. Danny's face was bloody around the eyes and mouth. It looked like his nose had bled a lot when he was killed and his moustache and beard was matted with it.

'Fuck, I can't do it.'

'Wait, you've got a knife. Just fucking stab him.'

'Oh yeah.'

Sticky took his knife out of his pocket and flicked it open. Priest saw the danger and retreated quickly.

He stood on the other side of the window, holding the axe in his hand, watching. Waiting.

'Stalemate,' said Sticky.

He flashed his knife a few times. Cocky, like he'd got one over on the famous serial killer.

'We need to take the hostages somewhere safer,' said Mills.

'Safer? Is a safe, safe?' said Sticky.

'Safe-safe, safe-safe-safe?' said Mills, being a twat.

Catherine was perched on a desk with her hands tied behind her back, but her mouth still ungagged. 'We'll run out of oxygen in the safe. We could blockade ourselves in the staff room. There's a pool table and a *Doctor Hammer* arcade machine in there.'

'At least we wouldn't be bored,' said Sticky.

'To put against the door, not to play, you idiot,' said Catherine.

'She called me an idiot,' said Sticky.

'You are an idiot,' said Mills.

'Isn't there a fire exit we can get out of?'

'The police will have it covered.'

'Right. Staff room then. Let's go.'

Mills untied the hostages while Sticky guarded the window with his knife.

Catherine walked the hostages down the back corridor that led to the staff room and toilets.

Mills went last and as soon as he got to the staff door, and everyone was inside, he called out to Sticky.

'Now.'

Sticky turned on his heel and ran. The moment he moved Nick Priest started worming his way through the tight cashier window.

CHAPTER NINE

Sticky leapt into the staff room and turned and slammed the door shut behind him.

Mills was ready with the heavy pool table. Catherine was helping to manoeuvre it in place, as best as she could with a wounded hand.

Sticky got behind it and helped them. They rammed it against the door just as Nick Priest got there and started pushing it open.

They stepped back and breathed a sigh of relief. Everybody in the room. All at once.

'Do you think that will hold him?' said Mills.

'I think we should put the arcade machine on there too,' said Sticky.

'Uh-huh,' said Catherine.

They watched the handle turn a few times. The door opened less than an inch and banged against the table. Not even enough to get a fingertip through. They gave the pool table another shove and the door banged shut.

Sticky pulled the arcade machine away from the wall.

'A pool table and arcade machine? I should have paid more

attention in maths. Staff room at the pub is just an empty keg with an ashtray on it.'

Mills helped drag it across the room. They tilted it against the pool table.

'Backs straight, knees bent,' said Mills.

They hefted it up and it fell back, landing with a THUD on the table. They climbed up, got it upright, and pushed it against the door.

Priest was standing outside the staff room. He looked at the axe and then at the door. Stared at the brass plate with the words, STAFF ROOM engraved on it. Considered smashing his way through but walked away.

He wandered back down the corridor. Looking all around, like a curious hen. Sat in the cashier's chair in front of the broken window. Looked down at the open cash drawer. Took out a stack of fivers. Looked down at the open duffle bag. Put them in on top of the cash that was already in there. Stared at the money. Felt nothing.

Meandered to the back stairwell. Looked down. Could hear Caine and Grey down there.

The phone rang.

He picked it up.

O'Neil's voice. 'So, do we have a deal. You let a hostage go and we'll talk about freedom.'

Priest looked at the main doors of the bank.

O'Neil continued. 'Are you there? Send someone out now and we'll know you're cooperating.'

Priest put the phone down and walked to the door leading to the foyer.

He moved the chair out of the way. The one that had been wedged there to keep him out. Went back out to the main foyer.

Stood before the main doors. They were big. Two-wide and went right up to the ceiling. Old building. He put his hand on the door handle and turned it.

Locked.

He looked up at the top of the door. The bolts were keeping it from opening. That's right. The one called Mills had bolted it shut.

Priest reached up and pulled a bolt free and caught sight of himself in the convex security mirror in the corner of the room.

His hand retreated from the second bolt, and he walked to the mirror and looked up. Stared at himself with his new face.

Reached up and pulled the mask from his head. Looked at it in his hands. A deformed profile. His own face was wet with blood.

He put the mask on the customer service desk while he took off the black coat he had taken from Danny's body.

Laid it on the floor under the convex security mirror. Arranged it neatly, even doing up the buttons. He placed the mask of Danny above it, facing up. Patted the beard down over the V of the collar. Stepped back and appraised it.

He picked up the axe and returned to the back area. To the stairs. To Caine and Grey.

CHAPTER TEN

Caine looked at his phone. Message from Charlie: 'Everything OK?'

He wrote a reply. 'No. Need an exit.'

Dominic turned the dial to its final number. 'Got it,' he said. He opened the little safe and removed two large keys. Stood up and walked to the main safe.

'Isn't the point of having two keys to keep them separate?' said Grey.

Dominic put the first key in the slot. 'Sure. And in 1900 when this was built two people would have had a key each so no single person could open it. But eventually convenience won out over security. And besides, we don't keep all that much money here these days.'

He put the second key in and turned them both together. There was a metal CLUNK as something moved inside the door. He turned the wheel and the huge door swung open.

Nick Priest stepped off the bottom step behind them. Watched. Quiet. Curious.

Caine looked up from his phone, saw him and looked down again. Looked up, having registered what he had seen.

He nudged Grey.

Grey looked. Dominic saw them and he looked too.

Priest was holding the axe on his shoulder like a baseball player posing for a photo.

Nobody spoke. Nobody moved.

Four men. Standing in a room. One with a bloody face.

Nobody spoke. Nobody moved.

Four men. Three of them staring at the fourth.

Nick smiled. A small smile. A terrifying one.

'Let's get in the safe,' said Dominic. Very quietly.

Caine and Grey nodded, imperceptibly. Stepped back as one.

Priest's face turned ugly. A sour deformity of features. He threw the axe and it struck Dominic hard in the face. His head snapped back. The axe stayed where it was. Looked like Pinocchio with a bad nosebleed.

Dominic tumbled to the floor.

'Shoot him,' said Grey.

Caine drew his gun and held it firm on Priest, who was now struggling to get control over a fit of giggles. He was holding his crotch like he might piss himself.

'Get on your knees, you fucking psycho,' said Caine.

Priest calmed down far too quickly. Obscene giggling schoolgirl to upright man, quick enough to make you flinch.

He started towards them, and Caine squeezed the trigger.

BLAM.

The shot was loud. Grey covered his ears and Priest covered his face and head with his arms. All motion ceased while Grey watched and waited to watch him fall to his death and Priest waited for the pain. Priest slowly lowered his arms. No bullet hole. No wound. No pain.

'What the fuck happened? Did you miss?' said Grey.

'Get in the safe,' said Caine.

They backed in fast and pulled the door shut. They turned the handle on the inside, locking themselves in.

CHAPTER ELEVEN

It was dark in the safe. Grey got his phone out and turned the torch on, illuminating their faces.

In the spread of the light the interior handle of the safe was visible.

'What the fuck happened?' said Grey.

'I'm loaded with blanks.'

'Why?'

'Because I'm not a hypocrite. Crime without victims, right? Nobody dies. I take what I say seriously.'

'Fuck me, Caine. And what if there happens to be a serial killer in the bank when you're robbin' it? Didn't you ever think of that?'

'Didn't I ever think of that? No? I also haven't planned for wild animals, sudden pandemic outbreaks, or cave-ins. This sort of shit doesn't usually happen when you're making a simple bank withdrawal.'

There was a CLUNK and the wheel in the safe door started to turn.

'We left the keys in the door,' they said, together.

They grabbed the wheel and turned it back. They held it

tight, leaning in, struggling, until they felt Priest give up.

They let go and watched the wheel.

Priest let go of the wheel and looked down at Dominic.

He put his foot on Dominic's chest and pulled the axe free from his face. The force of the withdrawal sent a splatter of blood against the safe and a few teeth tumbled out of his mouth.

Using the axe blade, he cut across the neck as far around as he could go and then rolled the body onto its front and continued the cut across the back of the neck.

He sliced up the centre to the crown of Dominic's head, flipped him back over and reached around and grabbed the two flaps of skin he had created. Put his foot back on Dominic's chest and pulled up. The skin rolled off the bone of his scalp and stopped above the brow.

Now he was more careful. He tore the skin away from the face of the skull with gentle tugs. He did it with practiced efficiency.

With the skull now completely de-gloved, he pulled the mask over his own head.

He stood there for a while, looking out through Dominic's eyes. Made some adjustments so his view wasn't obscured by the bank manager's eyelashes.

There was a raw, jagged cut down the centre of the face where the axe had struck. The nose was cut in two and Priest's own nose protruded through it.

He looked down at Dominic's clothes, then knelt and

started unbuttoning Dominic's uniform.

Priest ran up the stairs like a kid, excited to show his mum his new Halloween outfit.

He ran from the back area out to the main foyer and across to the private office and entered. Stepped over Danny's body to the desk where he knew there was a rectangular chrome vase, holding fake flowers.

He put the vase on the printer and stood back to admire himself in the reflection. He turned and looked at himself in different angles. Stood proud. Hands on hips.

Having satisfied his vanity, he left the room and wandered aimlessly as he made his way back to the back area.

He touched things. Absently pressing keys on keyboards. Taking notes out of an open till and letting them flutter to the floor. Sat and spun in an office swivel chair. His head fell back, and he watched the ceiling spin. He slowed and stopped. Tutted. Looked over at the corridor that led to the staff room.

He stood outside the staff room door. Poked it with a finger.

There was a filing cabinet in the corridor on the far side of the staff room door. He looked at it for a moment, thinking. He crouched down behind it.

CHAPTER TWELVE

Sticky climbed down from the pool table with the plug for the arcade machine in his hand. Had found an extension lead and plugged it into the wall. It reached as far as the pool table legs. He plugged it in.

It started up with an 8-bit jingle.

'Do you think we should be trying to solve the whole "being trapped in a bank we're trying to rob while being hunted down by a serial killer" thing before we start playing games, Sticky?'

'You work on that. I'll play *Doctor Hammer*.'

'Or, one or both of you brave men could go out there and stop him,' said Catherine.

'You can go out there if you want. I'm staying in here until we hear from Caine.'

'That's if The Mask Collector hasn't killed them already.'

The hostages had all been left untied but given strict orders to keep the gags on. They were, after all, still hostages. Not their fault there was a maniac in the middle of the gang's noble bank-robbing plans.

One of the hostages—a guy named Trev, wearing a black

and red Shelley Town FC football shirt—tore the gaffer tape off and pulled the tie out of his mouth.

'Can we take these off now?' he said.

Mills and Sticky turned to him. 'No,' they said, as one.

A few of the other hostages had started taking theirs off. They stopped and patted the tape back down, shrugging at each other in a, *it was worth a try*, sort of way.

'Alright, I'll put it back on, but hear me out first.'

Mills and Sticky didn't say anything. They looked at him patiently, waiting for him to continue.

'If you stop that psycho out there the papers will hail you as heroes and the judge will probably let you go for the bungled robbery.'

'Go out there and stop him?' said Mills. 'What do you think, Sticky?'

'I don't know, Mills, what do you think?'

'Thank you for asking, Sticky. Here's what I think. I've been in a lot of fights in my time, how about you Sticky?'

'I've been in a fair few fights in my time, Mills, I'm always eager to jump in when one breaks out down the pub, how about you, Mills?'

'Sticky, I'm the same. Nothing like a good punch up after a pint. And what have we learned from our experiences in that field?'

'Is it the thing about fighting with that one in a hundred person who is actually a genuine psychopath?'

'That's it, yes.'

'Well, in my experience, it doesn't matter how hard you

punch. If the guy you're fighting is willing to break a glass and stab you in the eyes with it, you make your excuses and walk away from the fight.'

'But Sticky, there's two of us, so we've got a good chance of winning.'

'Yes, but our own psychopath, Danny, got in a fight with him, and that didn't go down too well.'

Mills raised his finger, as though making a point. 'Can we conclude then, that if we take him on there is a very good chance that one or both of us will have our faces peeled off?'

'I think that's safe to say.'

'Would you like to have your face peeled off, Sticky?'

'No thank you, Mills.'

'How about you, Mr. Hostage?'

Trev looked down. 'No thanks.'

'Alright then. We'll wait for Caine to call. Put your tape back on and sit in the corner with the rest.'

'You know what you could do, though?' said Trev.

'What's that?'

'Find out who he is. You must be curious? The papers have been speculating for months.'

'How? Check his pockets?' said Mills.

'He banks here, right? His details would be on the computer. If you find it you could call the police and tell them his name, start on your journey to becoming heroes. You know? Maybe just addressing him by his name will catch him off guard. Take away his anonymity, or something.'

'We would need to know his name or account details to be

able to look him up, clever bollocks,' said Sticky.

'You wouldn't. She—' Trev looked at Catherine, 'was helping him when you came in. His details will still be open on her computer screen. Right?'

Catherine thought about it. 'Yes. He's right.'

'I don't think we would gain anything by knowing his name. It's not going to stop him from killing us,' said Mills.

'Maybe he's onto something though. Think about it. Our faces are all over the CCTV. We're nicked whatever happens. What if we could go out those front doors with The Mask Collector caught? It would change everything,' said Sticky.

Mills thought it over.

'Between us we've got one shitty knife. If we're going out there at all we're going to need something with a bit more reach.'

They looked around the room and both their eyes settled on the rack of pool cues on the wall. They looked at each other and shared a shrug.

'If it comes to it, we'll pub-fight him to death,' said Sticky.

'We'll have to tie the hostages back up. Can't have them running amok while we're busy saving the day.'

CHAPTER THIRTEEN

Caine and Grey were filling their duffle bags with money, illuminating the safe with the torch on Grey's phone.

They zipped up the bags and put their ears to the safe door, listening for The Mask Collector.

'I'm going out there,' said Caine.

'To do what? Throw your gun at him?'

'Ha ha. I didn't see you getting your machetes out.'

'And do what with them? Run up to him and chop him up? This isn't a movie. I ain't hacking no one to bits. I've got a grandmother. I visit her. We drink tea. I have barbecues on the weekends. I watch *Britain's Got Talent* and eat a roast on Sundays. I'm a normal bloke. Alright, sometimes I rob banks, but I don't go around lopping people's arms off.'

'Then why bring them?'

'Because they're fucking scary. Same reason you carry the gun. Like you say, no victims. It's an honest crime.'

'I'm starting to realise how mad that sounds.'

The safe door slowly opened and pushed against Dominic's body. Caine's head peered out and looked around. Boxes of leaflets, a small safe with cups and a hand of cards on top, two wooden chairs; not a single face-removing hobbyist in sight.

'Okay, we're safe,' he said.

'I don't know about your idea of safe, Pat.'

Caine looked back at Grey. 'I wasn't immediately murdered when I poked my head out for a nosey.'

'Safe enough. What's the plan?'

'Fucked if I know. He's probably busy killing the others. Maybe we can grab a bag of money and get out a window or something.'

'We've got to face it, man, this robbery is over.'

'Says you,' said Caine. 'I have no desire to A: Go to prison again. Or B: Get my face ripped off. So we're getting the fuck away from here, and then the fuck out of the country, and we're going to need all this money to do it. Either that or we'll be getting jobs picking fruit when we land as illegal immigrants in whatever foreign paradise we escape to.'

'I don't think they've got fruit picking at Strangeways.'

'Ha ha.'

Caine thought for a moment.

'Fuck,' he said.

'What?'

'Why do I have to be such a nice guy, Grey?'

'You're not a nice guy, Pat. You're a crook and a womaniser.'

'Fuck off. Alright, we need to regroup and get Sticky and Mills and the rest of those stupid fucking hostages out of here safely somehow and then still find a way to escape with the money. Right?'

'Sure, Caine. Whatever you say.'

Mills and Sticky were coming down the corridor with their pool cues cocked like baseball bats. Catherine was close behind them.

They edged into the back area and looked around cagily.

'You see him?' said Mills.

'No, you?' said Sticky.

'No.'

There was a noise from the stairwell. It had the effect of a freeze-ray. Like in a science fiction film. One moment they were edging forwards. The next, statues.

'You hear that?' said Sticky.

'Yeah.'

They hushed Catherine, unnecessarily, and she rolled her eyes. They crept backwards like cartoon robbers with swag bags. Stopped when they were out of sight. Sticky's pool cue tapped the wall by accident and Mills looked back at him, every inch of his face in a *Do you want to get us killed?* expression. He was met with Sticky's apologetic grimace.

Caine and Grey came up the stairs and stepped into the back area.

'I think I heard something,' said Grey.

'Where?'

Grey nodded in the direction of the staff area, and gripped his machete handle a little tighter.

Mills, Sticky, and Catherine hid against the wall and listened intently.

'Is it him?' said Sticky.

'Shut up,' said Mills.

Behind them, The Mask Collector snuck out from behind the filing cabinet and let himself into the staff room.

'Who's back there?' came Caine's voice from the stairwell.

'Caine?' said Mills.

'Mills? Where is he?'

'Fuck knows? He's not back here.'

Grey stepped into the corridor in front of Mills, like a Māori haka. Big grin on his face, wielding both machetes.

'Boo.'

Mills and Sticky fell backwards, and Mills swung wildly, as if he was being attacked by seagulls. He realised it was Grey and the scare wore off.

'Jesus, shit!'

'Fuck off, you cunt,' said Sticky.

Grey laughed. 'Alright, shh. Shut up. He might hear us.'

'And whose fucking fault is that?' said Sticky.

'You're a bunch of children,' said Catherine.

Mills walked out to the main back area and Sticky followed.

Caine was looking through the smashed cashier window, making sure Priest wasn't ducked down on the other side.

'Where is he?' he said.

'Isn't she supposed to be tied up?' said Grey.

'We need her help,' said Mills.

'Help with what?' said Caine.

CHAPTER FOURTEEN

Priest closed the door behind him and looked at the hostages.

The hostages were huddled in the corner facing away from each other in a circle, tied together by the hands.

They started to panic. The ones who were facing away from Priest could hear the panic but couldn't see the cause. They twisted around to see.

There was Nick Priest, wearing Dominic's uniform and face.

He walked around them like a sergeant inspecting his troops. Stopped in front of Trev. Touched his chest. Ran a finger down his belly.

Trev flinched away, almost causing the huddle to fall over.

A muffled scream started to travel around the group as the fear came over each of them in turn. They screamed louder to try and draw the attention of the bank robbers, but they could only make desperate muffled sounds under their gags.

Half of the hostages were customers; the other half were members of staff. Employees of the bank. Dominic had been their manager, their friend. They had gone for work drinks with him. A few had been at his baby shower, congratulated his pregnant wife.

Now Nick Priest's hot breath spilled out of Dominic's torn lips.

Priest stopped in front of each person. Enjoying this rare and strange luxury of having so many victims so kindly prepared for him. He kissed a girl. The youngest in the group. Had student written all over her. Pulled the gaffer tape off but left the gag in.

The split dead skin of Dominic's lips touched against hers. She twisted her head away. Her face scrunched up so hard it hurt. Lips clamped shut around the fabric of the tie. The smell was awful. It didn't smell like death, maybe that would have been better. It smelled like fresh uncooked bacon.

Priest held her head with both hands and turned her face with force. Pushed his lips against hers. Forced his tongue between her tight lips.

She looked. Couldn't help it. Her eyes opened just for a fraction of a second. The mask had shifted up, so Priest's eyes were no longer aligned. Dominic's eyelids were contorted upwards.

She scrunched her eyes back up. But even so, tears found their way out.

He let go of her. Put the tape back.

The next one in line was a man. Looked like a business guy. His face was calm. Trying to keep composed like he was in a high-pressure meeting. Poker face. Priest removed his tape. Gave him the same affection he had given the girl. Came in slow. The man didn't move. Priest lightly kissed his lips.

The man flinched. Aha, a reaction. Business guy's breath smelled of wine and tuna. Business lunch maybe. Business, business, business.

Priest moved on. Touched the breast of a cashier like he was testing a horn.

Squeezed the balls of a man like he was testing fruit. Looked like he could be the dad of the teenager.

Came to a woman who looked Spanish, maybe.

Looked at her for a while. She was afraid in an unbelievably pretty way. Sometimes fear was elegant in its purity. He didn't have a camera for a photo. Was disappointed he wouldn't have a permanent record of such ideal terror. He pulled his arm so far back it looked like he was trying to pick something up off the floor behind him, then slapped her so hard, a clump of mascara flew off her lashes.

Priest carried on his inspection and stopped when he came to a thin, tall woman wearing the same uniform as himself. The ugly green waistcoat, grey trouser, and white shirt.

He looked her up and down. She had short stylish hair. He untied her from the group and freed her hands. Unbuttoned her waistcoat and removed it from her.

Found a roll of gaffer tape on the floor and started taping her torso up, flattening her breasts.

He took off his own bloody waistcoat and swapped it with her. Now she was wearing Dominic's bloody uniform and he was wearing her clean one.

He tied her hands behind her back. Took off his shoes and then knelt and started removing her heels without informing her of his plan. Simply lifted her left foot off the ground from behind her and started trying to pull it off. She struggled, hopped as he pulled, and fell forwards.

With her hands tied she was not able to stop her fall. Her face bounced off the carpeted floor and her nose split with a horrible crunch. She rolled over on her back and Priest removed her other shoe.

He took Dominic's shoes off his own feet and put them on hers and then pulled her upright by the armpit.

Blood poured from her nose and ran down her chin and neck.

Priest removed Dominic's face, revealing his own bloody features, and stepped towards the girl.

He put the dead man's face over hers. It was wet against her face. Led her to the door. She started shaking her head in panic as it began to dawn on her what Priest was planning.

He opened the door and let her out into the corridor and quietly closed the door behind her.

CHAPTER FIFTEEN

EVERYONE was being as quiet as they could. Speaking in whispers.

'That's actually not a shit idea, Sticky. Grey, you go out with her and take a picture of the screen with your phone. It will be quicker than writing it down,' said Caine.

'Come on,' said Grey.

They went to the door that led out to the main foyer. Cautious. Grey checked behind the door. No psychopaths. They went out to the customer service desk.

They had figured he was in the private offices. There was nowhere else he could be.

Caine stood over the threshold between the foyer and back area and watched the private office door, ready to shout if it opened so Grey and Catherine could run back through, and he could slam the door after them and barricade it. Caine figured Priest wouldn't attempt to come through the window, it would be too dangerous for him.

Sticky and Mills hung back by the corridor. Pool cues held casually against their shoulders.

Behind them, the hostage girl, wearing Dominic's face,

approached slowly, trying to get their attention without startling them.

Catherine touched a key on the keyboard and the screen came to life.

Grey stood with his back to her, a machete in hand, keeping guard.

The computer asked for a password.

'What were you helping him with?' said Grey.

'He was opening a joint account with his wife.'

'He was married?'

She shrugged.

Grey glanced at the screen and nodded, trying to hurry her up.

He looked back and scanned the foyer. Something caught his eye. A black corner of cloth. He frowned and stepped sideways to get a better look. A black coat came into view. He stepped out further. Saw Danny's face, flat on the ground, staring up with vacant eyelids.

Grey's face saddened. His chest deflated as he let out a sigh of grief. There was no time for it. Stepped back to Catherine. Put it out of his mind. Focused on the now.

Catherine typed in a password, holding her wounded hand against her chest, and pressed enter. Red letters appeared on the screen.

INCORRECT PASSWORD. TWO ATTEMPTS REMAINING.

Grey gave her a sideways look.

'Come on, are you kidding?'

She typed the password again. The red letters changed.

INCORRECT PASSWORD. ONE ATTEMPT REMAINING.

'What the fuck are you doing? Put the password in.'

She stared at the keyboard. Typed a password. It was correct.

The screen changed and Priest's account came up. It was still there from when she had been helping him when Caine and the gang busted in and held up the bank.

Grey took his phone from his pocket and opened the camera function. Took a snap of the screen and checked the picture. It was clear. No blur.

The name of The Mask Collector was on the screen. The name the police and newspapers and victim's families had been waiting for.

'Nick Priest.' said Grey. 'Come on.'

They hurried to the back area and Caine quietly closed the door behind them.

Caine put the chair up against the door handle to wedge it shut and bolted the door at the top.

'What the hell was that?' said Grey.

'Sorry, nerves I guess,' said Catherine.

Grey wasn't convinced. He looked over at Mills, was about to say something. Stopped. Saw the girl wearing Dominic's face coming up behind Mills and Sticky.

'Behind you,' he said.

CHAPTER SIXTEEN

MILLS and Sticky turned around. There he was. The Mask Collector. In all his violent glory. Shuffling towards them with his hands behind his back. Making weird noises. Walking like his shoes were too big for him.

No time to assess the situation properly.

'Oh, fuck,' said Sticky, and swung. He struck The Mask Collector hard across the face with the thin end of the cue, tearing a slash into the cheek of the mask. He fell heavily sideways. Hit his head on the wall. Collapsed backwards. Unconscious. Nobody noticed that The Mask Collector's hands were tied.

Sticky jumped back, holding his cue ready to attack again if The Mask Collector got back up.

'I got him,' he said.

Mills stepped in.

'This is for Danny, you cunt.'

He held the cue up high and hit The Mask Collector hard across the legs, shattering one of his knees.

The girl, who was not The Mask Collector, balled up into a tight foetal position and yelled through her gag. A shattered knee is a reliable way to bring somebody back from unconsciousness. It didn't last long. The pain split through her, ground its way along her nervous system, hit her brain like an off switch. Her head bobbed back, and her tight position loosened. Unconscious again.

Caine and Grey joined them and looked down at the infamous killer.

Catherine stayed back. Her hand over her mouth, welling up.

Mills stood over the girl. Raised the cue up high with both hands, the thin end pointing down. Ready to stab The Mask Collector through the head.

'Don't you kill him. We don't do that,' said Caine. 'If you kill him, you're no better than he is.'

Mills didn't listen. Couldn't. Memories of Danny filled him, painted red. His anger was wrapped in grief. There was no getting through to him.

The Mask Collector moved again. Just a twitch. A sliver of life clambering to the surface.

Doubt had been dawning over Grey. He had been looking at the body closely. Something wasn't right. Now he could see it.

Mills took a hard short breath and brought the cue down.

Grey rushed forwards and pushed Mills into the wall.

The cue missed and struck the edge of the skirting board. It snapped at the end and Mills fell to the floor.

'It's not him,' said Grey.

'What?' said Mills, his eyes wide and fixed on Grey, looking for an explanation.

Caine stepped forward and pulled Dominic's face away from the battered bank employee.

Her face was badly bruised. She had a black eye and was bleeding from the mouth and nose.

'It's Rachel,' said Catherine.

Sticky got down on his knees and tried to gently wake her. 'Oh fuck, I did that. Shit, are you okay?' He shook her by the shoulder.

Grey looked at Caine. 'You might want to put that down.'

'What?' said Caine.

'You're holding a dead man's face.'

Caine looked at it in his hand. Recoiled slightly. Looked around for somewhere to put it.

'Where do I put this?'

Grey thought for a moment and came up short. 'Fuck knows.'

Caine carried it off like a dirty rag and laid it flat on a desk.

'She's breathing,' said Mills.

'Fucking wake her up then,' said Sticky.

'Calm down, mate. You might have hurt her, but I nearly killed her. We didn't know. Roll her onto her side.'

'Why?'

'Because that's what you're meant to do.'

They untied her hands and put her in something approximating the recovery position.

'Where did she come from?' said Caine.

Mills and Sticky looked at each other and then up at Caine.

'The staff room,' they said together.

'So, where's The Mask Collector?'

Mills and Sticky looked at each other again and then down the corridor.

'Staff room,' they said.

They all look down the corridor, at the closed staff room door.

CHAPTER SEVENTEEN

STICKY, Caine, and Grey, faced the staff room door, contemplating it.

Mills stayed back with the girl, touching her forehead with a wad of hand towels from the staff toilets. No idea why. Wasn't sure what else to do.

A closed door. Beyond it, a room full of bound and gagged hostages, and one of the most dangerous serial killers in history.

'Well, they're all dead,' said Sticky.

'What do we do here then, Pat?' said Grey.

'You want to open the door? You're the one with the machetes.'

They both looked at Grey, waiting for him to do something.

He took one of the machetes out of an inner pocket and took the door by the handle.

They waited. Grey didn't do anything. They waited a bit longer.

'You going to do something?' said Sticky.

He pulled the handle down and pushed the door open. It

swung gently away from them, revealing the room like a proud hand.

First, the right far corner. It was red with blood. Like somebody had taken a bucket of the stuff and sloshed it against the walls and floor. Trev was in the middle of it. His face was a skull-grin, unblinking eyes that moved in their sockets, muscles visible on his cheeks, stretching and tightening with the agony. He had been de-gloved, alive. His stomach had been sliced open and he was slowly bleeding to death. A pencil had been stuck into his throat. His breathing came short and raspy.

They looked at the scene with wide eyes and slack jaws.

The door continued its serene journey, and the rest of the room came into view.

In the middle of the room, The Mask Collector had arranged the rest of the hostages into a throne, like an amateur acrobatic formation. All still breathing.

Nick Priest was sitting, all casual-like, with his right foot rested on his left knee and his arms on the human armrests.

He was wearing Trev's face and football shirt.

Sticky leaned in and closed the door again.

'Yeah, fuck that,' he said.

Grey took out his second machete, so he had one in each hand.

'If we don't go in there, they're all dead.'

He looked Caine in the eye. Caine gave a nod. Grey nodded back.

Caine took the handle in his hand. He was about to push

but stopped.

'What's his name?'

'Nick Priest,' said Grey.

Caine pushed the door open.

Now the throne was gone, and the hostages had been arranged in a row, dividing the room in two.

Behind the hostages, Priest stood with the axe held lazily at his side.

They entered the staff room cautiously.

Catherine watched from the doorway. Curiosity on her face, but no fear.

Caine stepped forward. Sticky and Grey hung back.

'Why are you doing this?' he said.

Priest didn't reply.

'Nick Priest?' said Caine.

Priest looked to his side and sighed. Looked like he was mildly pissed off. Frustrated. Churlish. He looked back at Caine.

'Why do *you* do this?' he said, reflecting the question back at Caine.

'I'm not doing anything.'

Priest thought before he spoke. Considered his words carefully. Motioned to the hostages between them.

'Are these your hostages or are they mine? We are on two sides of the same act. We both hold the same hostages in aid of crime.'

'We are not the same. You're a psychopath.'

'Do you think normal people hold up banks? I would

venture that there are some psychopathic tendencies in you too. At least I am not afraid to embrace what I am.'

'I don't hurt anyone.'

'Hurt is not restricted to physical violence. You hurt people in a way that can't be seen.'

'I'm giving them a story they'll be telling for the rest of their lives. You're killing them.'

'You could have let them go. Given yourself up to the police. You had the chance. You put crime ahead of their lives. They mean as little to you as they do to me. Admit it.'

'You know, they'll probably bring the death sentence back for you.'

'No, they won't. Journalists will fawn over me. There will be books, movies, action figures.'

'You think any of those cops won't take the opportunity to shoot you on sight when they rush in here?'

'I'll be completely naked, covered in blood, surrounded by bodies. My arms in the air, jovially awaiting my arrest. They won't shoot me. I won't be a threat. I'll just be a naked lunatic.'

'Surrounded with bodies? You're not killing another person. We aren't going to let you.'

Priest nodded, considered the idea. Weighed its merits. Decided the statement was false and proceeded to prove it.

The hostage in the middle row was the teenager who had fallen over when Caine and his gang first entered the bank.

Priest moved suddenly. Swung the axe back in a sideways arc, like a professional hammer thrower, and hit the kid in the back of the head at the base of the skull. The gaffer tape that covered his mouth split open and the axe blade pierced through. Blood sprayed across the room and spattered Caine's shoes. He stepped back. The three of them did, in an instinctive retreat.

Priest yanked the axe out and the kid fell to the ground. The top half of his head was almost all the way off, it hung there by threads, held together by the tie and gaffer tape that had been his gag.

'What were you saying?' said Priest.

The hostages made a break for it. Filtered around Caine, Sticky, and Grey, like rocks in a river.

Priest let them go.

'When you're ready, Grey,' said Caine.

Grey cocked a machete and aimed.

CHAPTER EIGHTEEN

Grey threw the machete. It looked good. Spun through the air and looked like it might strike Priest in the face.

Priest watched it turn in the air towards him. Didn't dive out of the way, or raise his arms, just watched.

It struck him in the shoulder by the hilt and clattered harmlessly to the ground.

Priest reached down and picked it up. Axe in one hand, machete in the other.

'Yeah, nice work, Grey. This is much better,' said Sticky.

'Fuck you. I don't see you doing anything.'

Priest's body language changed. It was instant and alarming. Hard to describe exactly what had changed in him but it was like the room had been filled with static. It made Caine feel the way a cat gets when it catches sight of something in its peripheral. Alert. All senses waiting for movement.

And then it came. Priest went from standing stiff to sprinting like he had been shoved.

'Fucking run, lads,' said Caine.

They made it out the door and slammed it behind them.

The axe smashed a hole through the door and was immediately pulled back out. The door opened and The Mask Collector came running out, knees high and arms pumping like a cartoon villain.

The phone was ringing as they ran through the back area and out to the foyer. Caine grabbed Mills by the shoulder of his coat and pulled him to his feet. Mills looked back, got the message, and ran with them.

Sticky saw his hammer on the desk and grabbed it on his way past.

Grey got to the door that separated the back area from the main foyer and kicked the chair out of the way and pulled the bolt down.

Priest went straight for the broken window, hoping to get ahead of them. Instead, it slowed him down, but only a bit.

Caine got to the main doors first. He unbolted them and pulled both doors open.

Outside, police officers and reporters were milling around. Nattering, waiting for orders, or anything interesting to happen. Pedestrians were taking selfies with the bank in the background.

The bank doors opened and Caine, Mills, Sticky, Grey, and Catherine, burst out into the street and stopped.

Behind them, Nick Priest halted in the entrance. Bloody. Weapon in each hand. Big grin.

The phone could still be heard ringing inside.

For a moment the police just stared at the four men and

the woman.

In the café, Iain O'Neil had a mobile phone to his ear. He looked out of the window, at the men in the road. Pat Caine. In the flesh. He put a tick next to the name. Hung up the phone. Stood up from the table. Necked the dregs of his coffee. Put the cup down.

He left the café and walked through the gaggle of police officers and stopped a few metres in front of Caine.

'Pat Caine,' said O'Neil.

'O'Neil?' said Pat Caine.

'That's right. What's happening here? Are you handing yourself in?'

Caine took the gun out of his pocket and aimed it at O'Neil. O'Neil took a step back.

Sticky looked down at his hammer. Looked behind him. At Priest just standing there. He turned around and walked back into the bank.

Mills and Grey watched him go, bemused.

Sticky walked in and stopped.

Caine still had his gun pointed at O'Neil. Grey and Mills watched Sticky.

'Are you coming to get me, little boy?' said Priest.

Sticky threw the hammer and it spun through the air and hit Priest solidly in the centre of the forehead. He fell back against the cashier desk and slumped to the ground.

Sticky rushed over, took the axe and machete from Priest, and casted them aside.

Mills and Grey looked at each other.

'Holy fuck,' said Grey.

Mills reached forward and tugged the back of Caine's coat.

'What are you doing?' said Caine.

'We're going back in, trust me.'

Grey grabbed Catherine by the arm, and they all walked backwards into the bank.

Mills closed the door and bolted them shut.

O'Neil looked at the woman police officer he had spoken to previously.

'What was that about?'

She shrugged.

O'Neil walked back to the café and took his seat at the table. Motioned at the barista for another coffee. Went to the recent calls list on his phone. Pressed the most recent number and put the phone to his ear.

CHAPTER NINETEEN

The phone on the desk, in the back area of the bank, started to ring.

'Is he dead?' said Caine.

Sticky shrugged. 'I don't know. I hit him pretty hard.'

'Let's put him in the safe,' said Caine.

Grey put his machete down on the cashier counter, where the glass was broken, so it would be accessible from either side should he need it.

He moved Priest away from the counter.

'Give me a hand.'

Sticky picked up both legs, one under each arm.

'Both of you,' said Grey.

Mills took one of the legs and Sticky held the other. Grey picked him up under the arms, in a bear hug, and they carried him out to the back area and down the stairs to the safe.

Grey entered backwards, so he didn't see Dominic's corpse right away. He had forgotten it was there. Sticky and Mills got it without warning. They hadn't been prepared. On any normal day, a guy like Grey would have remembered that a room they were entering had a dead body in it. But today had been somewhat heavy on the death front.

'Oh God, what the hell?' said Sticky.

'Oh, yeah. This creepy little fucker's handiwork.'

'You could have warned us,' said Mills. 'What did you do? Hide in the safe?'

'Yes,' said Grey.

'Fair enough.'

'I would have stayed in there,' said Sticky.

Grey held Priest against him with one arm and twisted to open the safe door.

The door opened and an intake of muffled gasps escaped it. Sounded like a bus coming to a stop.

'What was that?' said Mills.

Grey turned to get a better grip on the handle, keeping Priest—still wearing Trev's face—close to his chest.

The door opened and they were met with the wide panicked eyes of the hostages. They screamed through their gags at the sight of The Mask Collector and tried to disappear farther into the safe, which was impossible considering they were already huddled against the back of it.

Scared the shit out of Mills and Sticky too. They screamed and Mills dropped the leg he had been holding.

'Fuck, I forgot about you lot,' said Grey.

Mills caught his breath. 'Why didn't you all escape out the front door when you had the chance?'

The hostages shared a look and then shrugged as a group.

'Bunch of fucking idiots,' said Sticky.

They carried Priest in, and the hostages filed out around

them. They dropped the unconscious Mask Collector on the floor without lowering him.

'Let's lock him in and hope the prick runs out of air before the cops get to him,' said Grey.

'Won't he be able to open it from the inside?' said Sticky.

'Not if it's locked from the outside. You lot need to get back to the staff room. You're safe now. This will all be over soon.'

They looked at Grey like visitors from another world.

'Move,' he said.

And they did. Spurred into action by his commanding voice, they hurried up the stairs.

Grey pushed the safe door shut and turned the keys to lock it.

CHAPTER TWENTY

The phone was still ringing. Caine slumped into the office chair beside it at the desk.

'This is a fucking nightmare,' he said.

He picked up the phone and put it to his ear. Saw the hostages coming up the stairs and pointed at them with a frown that clearly meant, *Shit, I forgot about them.*

Mills walked the hostages back to the staff room.

Grey and Sticky came up from the stairwell and stood around the desk to listen to Caine's phone call.

'O'Neil?'

'Are you ready to talk?' said O'Neil.

'You're going to make a deal with me.'

'Is that right?'

Caine thought for a moment. Looked at the girl on the floor at the end of the corridor, still unconscious.

'We're going to let the hostages go. And you're going to drop all charges against us.'

'Just like that? I know you're not an idiot, Caine. I've read your book. You know how this works. You can't just hand the hostages back and walk away.'

Mills returned from the staff room and sat on the corner of the desk to listen with the others.

'In exchange for our freedom, I'm going to give you something you want more than me.'

'Alright, I'll humour you. What do you think you have that is so great we'll just let you go?'

'The Mask Collector. I have his address and name.'

There was silence on the line for a beat.

'What?'

'If you want it, you just let me know. But I want it in writing that me and my lot will go free once this is over.'

'Alright, so what's his name?'

'No, that's not how this works. You get a judge, or whoever the fuck you need, to sign something to say we ain't going to prison, and the info is yours.'

'Just for the record, I think you're creating some bullshit to buy yourself more time.'

'It doesn't really matter what you think. But ask yourself this, if I'm telling the truth do you want to be the guy who delays his arrest?'

'Alright, I'll play. But I'm not a fool. When we've done our bit of running around to made-up addresses for you, you'll be back to square one. You'll be going to prison for the rest of your life.'

'Does holding up a bank come with a life sentence now?'

'It wouldn't make any difference if it did. You must be pushing eighty. Three months in prison would be a life sentence.'

'That's not a very nice thing to say, O'Neil, don't they teach you about ageism in your line of work?'

'Just give me the address so we can get this over with.'

'Get me it in writing and I will. And you should start taking this seriously. I'm not fucking around here.'

Caine hung up and looked at his colleagues with his old charming smile.

'I think this might actually work,' said Grey.

O'Neil put the phone down and looked at the far wall. His mind elsewhere. Running the conversation back over again in his mind. He stood up and left the café. Walked through the crowd to the front of the police line where the policewoman he had spoken to earlier was talking to a reporter.

O'Neil had no interest in the goings on of TV people. He took the policewoman by the arm and moved her out of shot, and earshot, of the reporter.

'Who's in charge of The Mask Collector case?'

'DCI Conrad.'

'Is he here?'

'He's a she. And no, she worked late last night. They found another body. She clocked off early this morning. She's probably asleep.'

O'Neil walked back to the café without thanking her.

The policewoman apologised to the reporter and continued her interview.

'At this point in time we don't know why Pat Caine has returned to robbing banks. We thought those times were behind him too.'

In the café, O'Neil made a call.

'It's O'Neil. I need you to put me through to DCI Conrad.'

CHAPTER TWENTY-ONE

DCI Conrad was squaring up to a bowling lane with the ball to her chin. She swung back and took her shot. The ball hit the floor with a THUD and drifted lazily into the gutter. She watched it roll slowly away from her. It missed all the pins and fell harmlessly into the abyss behind them.

'I am shit at bowling,' she said.

A man (her date, who had a name, she figured. Probably. Most people do. Maybe he'd even told her what it was. Who knew?) came up behind her with another ball. He put his arms around her.

'Here, let me show you,' said Date.

She squirmed out of his embrace.

'Get the fuck away from me with that rom-com shit. Give me that. I can bowl just fine.'

She took the ball in both hands and walked onto the bowling lane.

A bowling alley employee came over (whose name she did know. It was Steven. He had introduced himself when he asked for her shoes. A transaction that didn't go particularly well. She was still wearing her own).

'Ma'am, you can't walk in the lanes.'

'Fuck off,' she said, loudly.

She stopped about three feet away from the pins and, holding the ball with both hands, swung it between her legs and chucked it at them. Strike.

Steven was now standing with her date.

'Excuse me, please can you get off the lane?'

Her phone rang in her pocket. The screen said, PRIVATE NUMBER. She put it to her ear.

'Who is it?'

She listened. Looked back at her date and Steven. Steven was fed up and making hand gestures. Date was suppressing a laugh.

'I'm on my way,' she said.

She walked back down the lane. Ignored Steven and Date and picked up her glass of wine.

'Bowling is a shit first date,' she said.

Date put his hands up to protest. 'You sent me a message on Tinder at eight a.m. and ordered me to take you on a date. It's not like there are any restaurants open this early.'

'You're lucky you're handsome.'

She left without saying anything else. All they could do was watch her go.

'She seems nice,' said Steven.

'Fuck off,' said Date.

Her car swerved and then found its lane again. She was driving with one hand on the steering wheel, the other holding the glass of wine. Squinting at the scene before her.

The high street was packed with police, ambulances, fire engines, reporters, pedestrians. It was a mess.

'What the fuck is this shit?' she said.

She got as close as she could and stopped the car in the middle of the road at the end of the police barrier.

'Conrad?' said a policeman.

'Where's this O'Neil prick?' she said, getting out of the car.

The policeman pointed towards the café.

'Thanks.'

'I would knock and wait for him to come out. He's a bit protective over his personal space.'

'Uh-huh.'

CHAPTER TWENTY-TWO

O'NEIL watched Conrad pass the window and go to the door. She tried the handle. It was locked.

He got up and walked to the door. Held up a hand, urging her to be patient while he turned the latch.

The moment he did, she pushed the door handle down and barged in.

'Why have you locked yourself in a café?'

O'Neil closed the door and turned to her. She was leaning against the counter with her glass of wine.

'Bit early for a drink, isn't it?'

'I was on a date.'

He looked at his watch.

'It's ten thirty-seven in the morning.'

'I clocked off at seven. This is my night-time. What's going on here?'

She motioned at the horde of emergency services outside.

'Bank robbery. Hostage situation.'

'Is The Mask Collector holding up the bank?'

O'Neil shrugged. 'It's possible. I suppose he could be one of Pat Caine's gang.'

Conrad raised her eyebrows. 'Pat Caine is back to robbing banks?'

'Apparently so.'

She smirked. 'Brilliant. How old is he now? Eighty? I had breakfast with him once. Or, well, he was having breakfast at that Rose Cottage Café place, down near the theatre, and I walked in for a full English and sat with him. Nice bloke. He gave me his hash brown.'

'Right. Well, now he's holding up a bank and claims to have the name and address of The Mask Collector.'

Her demeanour became serious.

'What? Then why are we fucking around here talking about this? Give me the details.'

'I don't have them. He's offering up the information in exchange for us letting him and his crew go without pressing charges.'

'So, what's the problem? Give him what he wants.'

'We don't know if he's even telling the truth. How would he have that information? Why would he know where The Mask Collector lives? How does he know his name? We have no reason to trust him at this point.'

'If he knows where The Mask Collector is, give him what he wants. If he's fucking with you, it doesn't make any difference anyway. You just arrest him, and nothing has changed apart from it's a bit later in the day than it would have been. And besides, it's Pat Caine. People aren't going to mind if you let their lovable local old rogue go free. What are you waiting for? Why have you wasted time asking me to come and meet you? I should be on my way to the address already.'

'Alright, fair point. I'll get something written up and authorised.'

'How long is that going to take?'

'Not long, twenty minutes maybe. I need to get it agreed by—'

'Jesus Christ.'

Conrad downed her wine and put the glass on the counter. She left the café, disregarding O'Neil with a flippant hand gesture, and stormed outside.

She pushed through the police and reporters, crossed the road, and marched up the steps to the bank.

She banged on the door with her fist.

'Pat Caine? Are you in there? Open the fucking door.'

She banged again.

CHAPTER TWENTY-THREE

CAINE and his crew—and Catherine—were sitting on the office swivel chairs, looking bored.

Sticky was flicking rubber bands at Grey. One bounced off his face. Grey levelled his eyes on Sticky. Knew it was pointless to engage him. That's what he wanted. They'd end up wrestling on the floor. God damned ADHD kid.

Mills was at the injured girl's side on the floor at the end of the corridor, dabbing a wet towel on her forehead.

BANG! BANG! BANG!

'Pat Caine,' came a muffled shout from beyond the doors.

'Who the fuck is that?' said Grey.

Caine got up, walked around to the foyer. Stopped momentarily—startled—when he saw Danny's jacket laid out on the floor, Danny's face folded neatly above the collar.

He looked away. Shook it off. That was an emotion to deal with later. He went to the door. Put his ear to it.

'Who's there?'

'Pat Caine?'

'Yes. And who are you?'

'Do you really have the name and address of The Mask

Collector?'

'Yes.'

'This is DCI Conrad. I'm in charge of The Mask Collector case. I need you to give me that information now so I can apprehend him.'

'Sorry sweetheart, I need a signed deal first.'

'Fuck.'

Caine waited for more, but she didn't continue. He looked back at the others. Shrugged with his mouth.

Everybody outside—and by now there must have been more than a hundred people counting all the emergency services, reporters, and randoms—watched Conrad storm back across the road and into the café. Looked at each other with reserved British shock when she slammed the door and started gesturing at O'Neil to hurry up.

He gestured at the document on his table. Had a pen in his right hand and his mobile phone to his ear.

Caine was still in the foyer. Looking down at Danny's face, which was out of sight of everyone in the back area.

Mills was watching him with interest.

'So why do they call you Sticky?' Catherine was saying.

'Because he's a thief,' said Grey.

Sticky held his hands up and wiggled his digits. 'Sticky fingers.'

'Aren't you all thieves?' she said.

Grey chuckled and Sticky shrugged.

'Maybe,' said Grey. 'But I wouldn't pinch a tenner out of my nan's purse just to buy a Barbie sticker album.'

'Alright, no. I only nicked off her once and it wasn't fucking Barbie, you old twat. It was Monster Asylum stickers. And I was ten.'

Mills got up and walked out to see what Caine was up to.

'Everything good?' he said, coming into the foyer.

He stopped. There it was. Danny's face. It looked awful. So real and recognisably Danny but disturbing in its flattened form. Faces should not exist in a different room to their arms and legs. It's just not natural.

'We should move it. Put it with the body,' said Caine.

Mills didn't reply at first. He stared at it. Looked away.

'Yeah, we should.'

'Do you want to do it? You were the only one Danny seemed to talk to. He liked you. I don't think he liked anyone else.'

'He wasn't a dangerous guy. I know people think he was, but he wasn't really. He was just practical.'

'We'll put that on his grave. Here lies Danny Bell. In life he was violently practical. In death he was used as a hat.'

'That's fucking dark, man.'

Grey and Sticky joined them.

'We moving him?' said Grey.

'I don't think I can do it,' said Mills.

'Sticky, you do it,' said Caine.

'Why me?'

'You're young and resilient.'

'You're old, so you won't have to carry the memory around with you for as long.'

'Fuck it,' said Mills.

He knelt and picked up the face by the beard and dropped it on the coat. He picked up the coat and carried the face in it like a hammock.

'Someone get the door.'

The private office was an abattoir. Red everywhere. A chrome vase on the printer with a bloody handprint on it. A hole in the plaster where the watercooler had been. The carpet was squelchy with blood. Danny's body in the middle of it all.

Mills awkwardly shook the face out of the coat and placed the coat over Danny's body, covering the skull.

He took a moment to reflect.

'Fuckin' hell mate. I'm sorry it went like this. This should have been an easy steal for us. Quick job. Line our pockets. We would have been travellin' round in that shitty van you had your eye on. Me and you knockin' about, sleepin' in the back, raisin' hell. If I could make it up to you I would. But you're sort of dead. So, I can't. I'll buy that van though, if they don't put me in the nick for the rest of my life. Alright, mate, I guess I'll see you at the funeral. Your funeral. Alright. Bye, mate.'

Caine, Sticky, and Grey were all waiting out in the foyer. Mills came out of the office, his head down.

There was a voice at the door. It was O'Neil's.

'Pat Caine?'

CHAPTER TWENTY-FOUR

THEY moved over to the door. Caine put his ear against it.

'Yeah?' said Caine.

The letter box flap clattered, and O'Neil pushed a folded piece of A4 through. It landed between Caine's feet.

He picked it up and unfolded it. A hand-written note. Signed at the bottom. Big O, big N, and a squiggle.

'Is this for real?'

'It's real,' said O'Neil.

'It's handwritten. How do I know it will hold up in court?'

'It will.'

Caine put his hand in his pocket and took out his phone. Noticed he had a new message.

It was from Charlie. An ambulance emoji followed by the laughing emoji.

Caine replied with a question mark and then clicked off WhatsApp and opened the voice recorder.

'Push the letter box open,' said Caine.

O'Neil did and Caine passed the note back through.

'I want to hear you say it. I'm recording you on my phone.'

'That's fine,' said O'Neil, taking the note. There was a brief pause while O'Neil got on his knees so he could speak clearly through the letter box, which he kept open with one hand.

Caine held the phone to the opening and pressed record.

There was a shake of the paper and then O'Neil spoke. 'I, Iain O'Neil, confirm that you, Pat Caine, and the rest of your crew, will not be charged with any crimes committed today. In exchange for this you, Pat Caine, will give me, Iain O'Neil, the name and location of the person responsible for the linked murders known by the newspapers as The Mask Collector.'

Caine stopped the recording and put the phone back in his pocket. O'Neil handed the note back through. Caine took it and folded it. Put it in his inside jacket pocket.

'Good.'

Grey opened the gallery on his phone and clicked on the image of the computer screen. Held it out for Caine to see.

'His name is Nick Priest. He lives on Vin Street. Number fourteen.'

'Got it,' said O'Neil, and the flap clattered shut.

O'Neil underlined what he'd written down and walked away from the door. He tore the page from the notepad and handed it to DCI Conrad.

She looked at it. 'Nick Priest? That's the guy?'

'Apparently so.'

She was already walking, almost running, back to her car. She stopped and turned to O'Neil.

'I need two of these cops. I'll meet them there. Make sure they are armed.'

She got in the car.

'You got it,' said O'Neil.

She started the engine and reversed fast down the road. Did a three-point turn, not caring about the curbs or other cars, and floored it. She turned at the end of the road and was gone.

O'Neil set about finding some armed officers to send after her.

Caine, Sticky, Mills, and Grey—and Catherine—were back on the swivel chairs.

'What now?' said Sticky.

'We wait,' said Caine.

'Do you think he's dead?'

'Priest?'

'I'm a murderer if he is,' said Sticky. He looked at the girl on the floor. 'If she dies, I'm down for two. Your deal won't cover that.'

Mills got off his chair and walked over to the girl. Knelt beside her. Put a hand on the girl's shoulder. 'She's breathing fine. She's just a bit knocked out.'

'Maybe we should check on Priest,' said Caine.

Grey got up to retrieve his machete from the cashier counter, where he'd left it.

It wasn't there.

He looked through the smashed window and saw a machete on the floor on the foyer side. Assumed it must have fallen off.

He walked around and picked it up.

CHAPTER TWENTY-FIVE

THE safe door was still locked shut from the outside.

'We're only opening it enough to get a look at him. See if he looks dead or not. He might be up and ready to pounce so I want all of you with your hands on the door ready to slam it shut if he does, alright?' said Caine.

Everyone got in place. Caine turned the keys. They heard the mechanism unlocking inside the door.

They braced themselves.

'You ready?' said Caine. He got a nod from all of them. 'Alright.'

He opened the door, just a crack. Enough to see inside. He peered in with one eye. At the bare floor of the safe. From his vantage he could only see a slice of it, but he was pretty sure that was where they would have left him.

'Where did you drop the body?' he said.

'In the middle,' said Grey.

Caine opened the door wider. Maybe four inches. Wide enough that he could see most of the floor.

'You there, Priest?' said Caine.

No answer. He pulled the door open a bit more and now

he could see the whole interior of the safe. Nowhere to hide. The Mask Collector wasn't in there. The safe was empty.

Caine opened it all the way and went in.

'Where the fuck is he?' he said.

'We dropped him right here,' said Mills, stepping in and motioning with both hands at the floor, like he was about to demonstrate a dive. 'Right there.'

'Well, he can't walk through steel. Where the fuck has he gone?'

'This is impossible,' said Grey, pacing. 'What is he? A fucking slasher movie villain? There's no way for him to get out of here.'

'If he's loose, we're fish in a barrel,' said Sticky, his eyes fearful towards the safe door. 'He could close it right now and lock us in.'

'Or come in here and skin us,' said Mills.

Grey held up his machete and got everyone behind him. They edged out of the safe. Faced the stairwell. All silent for a moment. Couldn't hear anything. No feet on the stairs.

'Come on,' said Grey.

They walked slowly and quietly up to the back office. Looked in, all as one. Like meerkats.

Catherine was leaning back on a chair.

'You okay?' said Caine.

She looked surprised. 'Yeah, you okay?'

'Have you seen Priest?'

Her face was blank. 'Not since you three carried him down to the safe.'

'Alright.'

They all stepped into the back offices and fanned past her. Headed to the corridor that led to the staff room. To the hostages.

'Is he not in there anymore?' said Catherine.

They entered the corridor. Approached the staff room. The door was closed. They trod quietly. Held their breaths to not make a sound.

They stopped outside the door and listened.

The white door, with the plaque that said STAFF ROOM on it, was a portal to something obscene. Sounds emitted from it. Muffled grunts. The occasional THUD, THUD.

The fear that came over Caine's crew was greater than it had been all day. They didn't know how long he had been alone with the hostages. Didn't know how he had got out of the safe.

In Sticky's imagination, Priest had taken on supernatural properties. Maybe all of them had that primal fear. The fear of the uncertain. The weird. The unexplainable.

The fear fell through them like a cold cloud. Made their skin tighten against their bones.

Caine pushed the door open.

The scene before them was backed by the cheery 8-bit music of the *Doctor Hammer* arcade machine.

Grey muttered the words, 'Ho-ly shi-t.'

They bore witness to a ballet of blood.

Priest had one of Grey's machetes and was freely murdering the bound and gagged hostages in a choreographed scene of utter violence. It was like a K-pop music video. All the bright colours, the blood, the dancing.

He was standing over one of the three hostages who were still alive, twirling the machete overhead. It was the teenage girl. The student. He rammed the blade into her breastbone and shucked her ribs open like an oyster. Her neck tensed with a muffled scream. Her throat was raw. The vein in her slender neck was thick and tense, like she had been screaming for an hour. They watched it lose that tension. Soften as the blood ran out of her. As her life ran out of her. She fell to her side and blood poured out of her open chest like a spilled bucket.

The unreal dance continued. Nick Priest sidestepped to another. The old guy. The businessman.

He was shaking his head. Pleading. Kneeling. Hands tied to his ankles behind his back.

Priest looked him over. Swayed from side to side. It wasn't clear if he was dancing to the 8-bit music or to the music in his head.

He made a violent decision. Dug the tip of the blade into the man's leg, right behind the kneecap. Tore right through his trousers. He stepped back and pointed. Bent over backwards and let out a howl of laughter.

'Stop,' said Caine.

Priest swivelled. Looked sad at the sight of Caine. Looked back down at the man. Pulled the machete forward like a lever. The kneecap popped out of its socket.

He smiled and nodded at the man encouragingly, as if they

were both getting the same kick out of it. The man screamed. The sound broke through the gag and tape like a shotgun blast.

Priest turned and faced Caine. He was wearing at least three faces, maybe more.

'Just stop,' said Caine.

CHAPTER TWENTY-SIX

DCI Conrad was standing at the end of Vin Street waiting for the other cops to show. The white road sign was behind her, low down on a two-feet brick wall that curved around the corner property.

She had imagined the home of The Mask Collector hundreds of times during the long investigation. Had spoken to profilers about what kind of person he might be. What economic background he might have. What part of town he most likely lived according to the locations of the bodies.

This didn't fit at all. This was middle-class contentment with a bow on it. There wasn't a car more than three years old on the whole street.

A police car pulled up and stopped. No lights. No siren. At least they weren't morons.

Two policemen got out.

'This is probably going to turn out to be fuck all,' said Conrad.

'Yeah. Probably,' said the one who had got out of the driver's side.

The other officer took a battering ram from the boot of the

car, and they walked up the road.

They got to number fourteen and walked quietly up the garden path.

They got to the door. He held the battering ram in place a few inches above the handle.

Conrad gave the signal. The police officer swung back and busted the door open. They put the battering ram down and entered the building, Conrad taking the lead.

The two police officers were armed with the standard Heckler & Kock Mp5. They were holding them in the safe position. Casual. Not running in with guns aimed and ready to kill. This was being treated as a serious matter, but likely one that was created by Caine to buy more time. Nobody wanted to charge into a kitchen and put the barrel of an automatic weapon in the face of somebody's innocent grandmother.

The house opened into a hallway. Staircase on the left, three doors leading to rooms. Conrad went right, with one of the officers joining her. The officer pointed the gun in the first room but kept it low, not wanting to injure anybody with accidental gunfire.

Living room. Two couches. One TV. One fireplace. French doors leading to a tidy garden. Cabinet full of Royal Doulton figurines. No people.

There were pictures of a married couple on the walls.

Conrad heard the second officer take the stairs, two at a time. That meant downstairs was clear.

'You go with him,' said Conrad.

The officer followed the order.

Conrad looked in the room opposite the lounge. It was a dining room. Shiny, elegant table, a wall-cabinet full of probably never used dinner sets. Not much else. It was also absent of residents.

The last room on the ground floor was opposite the bottom of the stairs. She went in. It was the kitchen. Full of kitchen stuff. The married couple in the pictures were not present. This did not feel like the house of a psychopath.

She found some letters on the kitchen table and picked one up. It was addressed to Mr and Mrs Priest. She put it down and spread the letters out to see if there was anything useful.

Nothing stood out.

A moment later the two officers came down the stairs and entered the kitchen.

'Clear,' said the first.

CHAPTER TWENTY-SEVEN

All the hostages but one was dead. Priest was covered head to toe in blood. Looked like he had been dipped in red wax. Three of the hostage's skulls had been skinned. Priest was wearing them all. They bulged around his head.

He had the axe in one hand and the machete in the other. Blood was dripping from the machete. He let go of the handle. It struck the carpet and stayed there, upright.

He pulled off the first mask he was wearing and dropped it on the floor. Grabbed the other two in a bunched fist and pulled them off too. Dropped them on top of the first.

He balanced the axe on its head next to him so he could remove Trev's football shirt.

Stood in the middle of the carnage. Eyes locked on Caine's.

Mills and Sticky edged backwards.

'All of you get back. I'm going to fucking kill him,' said Grey.

Priest picked up the axe and ran forwards.

Caine, Sticky, and Mills fucked off. No hesitation. Grey stood his ground.

The blood splashed under Priest's feet. He swung the axe.

Grey kicked Priest in the groin. Damn hard too. Full weight, like he was trying to volley a ball over a house. He was sure he felt one of the maniac's nuts POP against his steel toe cap. If it did, Priest didn't react to it, but it did put him off his stride.

The axe blow missed and Priest fell awkwardly past Grey and out into the corridor. He stumbled. Steadied himself against the wall and turned back to face Grey.

Grey was right there with the machete coming down on him.

There wasn't enough room for Priest to swing the axe, but he managed to heft the head up as hard as he could and caught Grey in the chin just as the machete was coming down.

Grey stumbled back and Priest got out from under him.

He saw his chance. Swung the axe sideways and chopped Grey with a solid blow to the lower back. He let go of the handle and smiled at the bizarre aspect of a tool sticking out of a body. It never got old.

Grey fell to the ground. Face first. Smacked the floor like a dropped slab of pork belly. Chin bounced off the rough carpet.

Priest stood next to him. Took the axe by the handle and pulled it free.

Grey's spine was split in two.

Priest lurched back into the staff room and grabbed the machete and then headed out after Caine and the others.

The surviving hostage was the Spanish woman. She moaned. Her feet were visible from the corridor. Squirming.

Trying to get away from the blood but whichever direction she crawled, bound and slow, she was crawling towards it. It was everywhere. It smeared her face. Saturated her clothes. Styled her hair.

This would be her nightmare, asleep and awake, for the rest of her life.

CHAPTER TWENTY-EIGHT

Conrad opened the pantry. Figured she was in the wrong house. It was just a wind up. She stood there with the door open. A look of puzzlement on her face.

There were no shelves. No tins. No packets of pasta. There was a door. A second one. At the back of the pantry.

She reached in. Turned the round brass handle. It opened towards her.

The officers were standing against the kitchen counter. They watched her walk into the pantry. Stepped away from the counter and followed her.

'It's a basement,' she said.

There was a string dangling at the top of the stairs. She pulled it. A strip light blinked on.

She stepped down onto the first step. Leaned down and looked in before going farther.

'Anybody down here?' she said.

Silence.

She took the stairs with caution and stepped onto an old rug at the bottom. The whole floor was a patchwork of Afghan carpets, covering bare cement.

It was furnished in an older style to the main house. Looked like a trendy café. Old leather couches and lampshades. Art on the walls. Quirky ornaments on shelves. An old cathode ray television set. A gramophone.

She walked around, taking it in. Taking her time. The officers were quiet behind her. There was something off about this room. Something in the air. A chill. But not a cold one. A sensory chill.

There was an old minibar, like Del Boy had in his flat. A hideously real mannequin behind it caused her to gasp before she saw the seam around its plastic wrists and realised what it was. In the poor light, its face looked real.

There was an art studio set up in the corner and a portrait on an easel. Realistic but stretched out of proportion.

The light was too dim to make out the details of things. She stepped closer to the portrait. Squinted.

Her eyes adjusted to the darkness.

'Conrad,' said one of the officers.

'What?' she said, leaning closer to the canvas. Something awful was dawning on her subconscious. A feeling of dread that rose from her stomach before arriving at her brain as a coherent thought.

'These aren't pictures,' said the officer.

She saw it. The painting on the canvas. Figured it had been made with thick strokes of oil paint. It was a face. A real one. She was close enough to see the individual eyelashes. The texture of the lips. The pores in the skin. The hair in the stretched nostrils.

She looked away from it and turned to where the other officers were. They were standing by the couch. Their torches on the pictures. The walls were decorated with faces.

Every colour, age, and sex.

They were aghast amidst the overwhelming presence of loss. Of death.

It was clear that the method for displaying the faces had improved over time. Some were crudely nailed up, some were framed, some were stretched over embroidery rings.

She turned on her torch and illuminated the mannequin behind the bar. It wore the face of a well-groomed man. The skin, hard and dry, like aged meat. Painted to give it life-like colour.

In the corner, by the television, was a teddy bear with the face of a baby pulled over its head.

One of the police officers spotted it. Put his hand to his mouth and vomited through his fingers.

Conrad kept moving past the art studio, to the back of the stairs. Found the killing room.

It was bloody from floor to ceiling. There was an array of weapons and torture implements on shelves and hanging from hooks. A wooden chair in the middle of the room with restraints on it. A camera set up on a tripod, facing the chair.

She took her phone from her pocket and put a call through to O'Neil.

It rang once.

'O'Neil, Pat Caine was right. How did he know?'

'Have you apprehended him?'

'No. He's not here. But we know who he is now. We'll get him.'

O'Neil put the phone down and looked out of the café window at the bank.

'How did you know?' he said to himself.

He dialled the number for the bank and put the phone to his ear. Got up and left the café.

CHAPTER TWENTY-NINE

Caine and Sticky were sitting on the floor, crouched against the cashier counter.

The phone in the back started to ring.

Sticky had his eyes scrunched shut. 'I'm scared, Caine.'

They could hear Nick Priest walking towards the door that separated the foyer from the back area.

Caine looked around for something they could use to defend themselves. Sticky's hammer was on the floor, two metres away on his right. Must have landed there after it hit Priest on the forehead.

He leaned over and grabbed it. Nudged Sticky.

Sticky opened his eyes and looked at him. Caine proffered the hammer. Sticky looked at it and then at Caine. Shook his head. Whatever bravery had compelled him to chuck it at Priest earlier had left. Caine forced it on him. Sticky took it.

He looked to his left. Priest's shadow glided out of the doorway.

Sticky rocked the hammer in his hand, feeling the weight of it. It was reassuringly heavy.

Priest stepped through the door.

Sticky summoned bravery with an improvised war cry. 'Come on you fucking cunt,' he shouted, and hit Priest in the shin of his right leg. Heard the bone CRACK into splinters.

Priest fell forwards in agony and landed facing them. He was holding the machete out in front of him. He didn't yell with the pain. His face seemed to defy the knowledge that his leg was fucked.

It felt to Sticky that even on the floor with a broken shin, the hammer would be ineffective against him.

In the back office, Mills climbed out from under a desk and ran back to the staff room.

He stopped at Grey's side.

'Oh shit, mate. Are you alive?'

'Yeah, I can't feel anything. Can't move.'

Mills saw the open wound in his spine and chose to lie.

'You'll be alright, mate. I just need to borrow this.'

He took the machete out of Grey's hand and ran quietly back to the cashier windows.

As he got close, he got low and stepped slowly, trying not to make a sound.

He got to the broken window. Held the machete by the blade. Leaned through.

'Caine. Got a present for you.'

Caine looked up, saw the handle hovering above his head. Took it. Got to his feet.

'Sticky.'

Sticky looked back. Saw they had the advantage. Got to his

feet and joined Caine at his side.

Caine pointed the blade at Priest.

Priest stood up. Put all his weight on both feet, feeling the full agony of the pain from his smashed shin and not caring. They could hear the splintered bone crunch in his leg.

Sticky and Caine stepped towards the main door of the bank in a wide semicircle away from Priest.

Priest moved in a painful limp to block them.

Mills crept into the foyer and moved behind Priest.

O'Neil banged on the door, and everyone looked towards the sound.

'Pat Caine? You were right. It was his address. You're a free man.'

'Actually, you're a dead man,' said Priest.

'I'm not dying today,' said Caine.

'Then you'll have to become like me, Pat Caine. Put your blade in me. Take my life.'

'You know something, I've been thinking about this rule of mine. Victimless crime. Not hurting anyone. To kill would make us no better than scum like you. It's not true, is it?'

'You've got it. You're not better than me. You're the same as me.'

'No. That's not it. Because this isn't for greed or personal gain.'

'So, what's it for.'

'It's because you're a cunt,' said Mills.

He shoved Priest forwards. Sticky tripped him, and Caine thrust the machete forwards.

The blade punctured Priest in the cheek just below his left eye. The force of the thrust, added to the weight and momentum of Priest's falling body, was enough for the blade to pierce clear through his head. The blade emerged from the base of his skull, glistening with blood.

Caine held him there for a moment, blood cascading over his hands, gripping the handle so tight his knuckles were white.

He stepped back, letting Priest's limp body fall to the floor.

O'Neil banged on the door again.

'Caine, are you there?'

The phone was still ringing.

Caine stepped back again. His face was white.

'Caine?' said Sticky.

'Oh fuck, mate,' said Mills.

They ran to Caine's side just as he fell to his knees. The machete Priest had been holding was sticking out of Caine's side.

They helped him to the floor gently.

Catherine came out of her hiding place; the same free-standing sign Priest had hidden behind, promoting security assured banking. She darted to Caine's side.

'There'll be ambulances outside, right?' said Sticky.

'Yeah, open the door. Quick,' said Mills.

Sticky got up and ran to the door. Unbolted them and swung them wide open. The sun flooded in.

O'Neil was standing there with his hand poised to knock again. His eyes were on Sticky's. Could see the trauma in his face. His attention was drawn away from Sticky by a groan and he saw Caine. And he saw Nick Priest.

Behind O'Neil a murmur started to spread through the gathered police and reporters. They were walking closer, craning their necks to look at the bloody scene in the bank.

Cameramen jostled for the best shots.

'What happened?' said O'Neil.

'The Mask Collector happened,' said Sticky. He turned and pointed at Priest on the floor. 'Nick Priest.'

O'Neil looked down at Caine, at the machete sticking out of his side. He turned to the gaggle behind him.

'Paramedics.'

CHAPTER THIRTY

THE bank swarmed with emergency services.

One of the paramedics treated the girl in the corridor. Still unconscious.

An officer threw up at the far end, beyond the staff room door, while two paramedics tended to Grey.

Grey nodded his head to something he was asked.

Officers and paramedics, plastic coverings on their shoes, checked the bodies in the staff room, looking for signs of life. Photographs were taken. The Spanish girl was found alive, but the triumphant feeling was quickly dampened by the constant presence of suffering.

Everyone was quiet and respectful. They looked around with their minds blank. Unable to comprehend the sheer volume of violence.

Caine and Priest were raised on gurneys.

Priest was unmoving.

Caine was awake but lying with his eyes closed.

'Are you allergic to anything?'

Caine opened his eyes. 'Just bananas,' he said.

'Are you okay with morphine?'

'I wouldn't turn it down.'

She started to prepare some pain relief.

O'Neil was on the phone, looking down at Priest's body. The machete was still sticking out of his face.

'We've got him,' he said.

'He's at the bank? One of Caine's crew?' said Conrad, down the line.

'No, he was just here by chance. One of the customers. They took him hostage with the rest of them and I guess he got free.'

'Is he speaking?'

'He's dead.'

'Shit.'

A man wearing a paramedic's uniform walked in and stopped in front of the main doors. It was Charlie. He assessed the situation. The duffle bags full of money, in a pile on his left. He looked at them and then at Caine on his gurney being administered an injection of morphine.

He looked at Mills and Sticky over by the private offices. Sticky was holding the door open, showing a policeman Danny's body.

Charlie looked back at Caine and then down at the money. No one was watching him. Everyone was too busy with the hectic crime scene.

He picked up a duffle bag like he was picking up a tool kit. Confident and perfectly normal. Just one of the team. He walked up to Caine and put the bag under the gurney.

'Is he ready to go?' he said to the female paramedic.

'I think so, are you—'

She was interrupted by a police officer calling through from the back area.

'Do we have any free paramedics? We need some help back here.'

'You go, I've got this,' said Charlie.

She gathered her things and shot off to help.

The gurney started moving. Caine, who'd had his eyes closed during this exchange, opened them and lifted his head to see where they were taking him.

He saw the hands that were pulling the gurney. Tattooed on the knuckles were the words, MOVE and FAST. The knuckles swollen and bloody.

'Charlie?' he said.

Charlie got Caine outside and down the disabled ramp. Caine tried to get a better look at him, but the morphine was making him want to sleep and the sun was right behind Charlie's head, making his face a brightly edged silhouette.

They turned onto the road and Caine was able to get a better look at him. Charlie's lip was split, and he had a black eye.

'What the fuck happened to you?'

'Paramedics are stronger than they look.'

'You know we don't actually need an escape plan now? We made a deal.'

'Does that deal involve you keeping the money?'

'No, of course not.'

'Sounds like you still need an escape plan then.'

They stopped at an ambulance parked at an angle beyond the police cordon. Charlie opened the back doors.

'I do need to go to the hospital, if you don't mind Charlie? Drop me off there and then go and hide the money somewhere.'

'You got it, boss.'

Catherine jogged over. 'Can I ride with you?'

They both looked at her. She pointed at her hand where Danny had stabbed her with the pen.

Charlie and Caine shared a look.

'Sure,' said Caine.

She got in the back of the ambulance and Charlie took the duffle bag from under the gurney.

Back at the bank, Priest was rolled down the steps. Paparazzi hustled around to take pictures.

CHAPTER THIRTY-ONE

CONRAD pulled on some latex gloves, the finishing touch to her protective clothing.

She turned to face the killing room in Nick Priest's basement. The camcorder was facing an empty chair.

She pressed a button and a video started to play on the small fold-out screen.

The Japanese tourist was sitting in the chair, bound at the wrists and ankles. He was naked. Very badly hurt, apart from the face, which was untouched.

Priest was there, from the shoulders down. His clothes stained with blood. Holding a knife.

A woman came into view, but her head too was out of shot. There were bloody tools on the worktop behind them. She picked up a chisel and a hammer. Looked at the victim for a moment. He mumbled something inaudible.

She put the chisel to his collarbone.

He looked up at her saying, 'No, no, no.'

She brought the hammer down on the chisel with an audible DINK, and the collar bone snapped in two.

The man screamed.

Priest walked past the camera and went behind it. Conrad shivered as if his ghost had just walked through her. He adjusted the camera angle, and the woman's bloody face came into view.

Conrad paused it. Took out her phone and took a picture of the screen.

Called O'Neil, put the phone to her ear and ran upstairs and into the kitchen. Rifled through the letters on the table and picked one up.

O'Neil answered the phone.

'O'Neil.'

'He didn't work alone, she helped. The Mask Collector isn't one person, it's two. Husband and wife. I'm sending you a picture.'

She pressed a few buttons on her phone and hit send.

Looked at the name on the letter.

'Her name is Catherine Priest.'

CHAPTER THIRTY-TWO

O'NEIL looked at the message on his phone. Zoomed in on Catherine's face.

'She was here.'

'What?' said Conrad, on the phone.

'She was here. She works here. She went—'

He walked outside. Looked down the road. Saw Charlie close the back doors of the ambulance and make his way around to the driver's side door.

'Hey, wait.'

Charlie looked at O'Neil. Paused for a moment, then got in the ambulance and pulled away from the curb.

'No, wait!'

The ambulance got almost to the end of the road and then jerked sideways. It swerved. Jerked the other way and then lost control completely and scraped against the cars parked along the road.

Everyone's attention was on the ambulance now. The whole audience. All the cops, the emergency services, pedestrians, reporters, paparazzi. Everybody was fixed on it. Tiptoes. Craned necks. A cameraman clambered onto the roof of his van to get a better shot.

The ambulance coasted across the tarmac, bumped up onto the curb, struck a pay and display meter and stopped.

The people watched in curious silence.

Nick Priest was lying on his gurney with the machete still in him. Not a single eye was on him.

Priest sat up.

The paramedic next to the gurney felt a hand on her shoulder. She looked at it. Her gaze followed the arm to its shoulder. And to the face. With the machete sticking out of it. She twisted out of his grasp and screamed.

The heads of every person in the crowd turned as one to see what the screaming was about. A communal gasp, and they recoiled from Priest all at once.

```
                                              CUT TO BLACK
                                              ROLL CREDITS
```

```
THE END
```

Extract from *The Threat of Violence* by Pat Caine. Published by Underhand Books, 2013.

Pages 1 – 4

I was born at a very young age. Ha-fucking-ha. Good one, right? I was always a charmer, that's what Mum told me. You want to call her a liar? You better be prepared to say it to my face.

Nah, I wouldn't hurt you. I'd never hurt a fly. But I've got some pretty dodgy mates who have become quite loyal to me over the years, so fair warning. To be honest though, most of them are in the nick. You know what, let's just shake hands and call it a day.

Listen, I'm not really that interested in sharing my childhood with you. It's not really for you and it's not all that interesting. Well, maybe I'll tell you one story. Sort of have to really. It was the first time I committed a crime.

Milk floats. They were designed to be robbed.

It was me and Roland Grey. 1964. We were both fourteen. Best mates then, best mates now. Known him since junior school when we were eight.

It was summer. Or winter. Or one of the other seasons. I wasn't keeping a diary at the time, and it was forty-six years ago. I'm only about eighty percent sure that it even happened. I'll run it by Grey in a bit, he might remember. You know what, I will ask him. Going to call him now. Don't get carried away and start reading another book, I won't be long.

Alright. He remembers it different. He thinks I was wearing shorts. I've never worn shorts my whole life.

It must have been summer because it was sunny. Funny how that works.

Milk float used to come by about 6am. You could hear the electric motor going.

I know what you're thinking, 'Oh, the great bank robber, Pat Caine, started his life of crime, pinching bottles of milk off the back of the float. I did that. Everyone did it.'

No, you just wait. We were doing that since we could walk. Doesn't even count as a crime. This was a whole different thing.

I remember we had arranged to meet halfway up the hill. I lived at the bottom, and he lived at the top.

He was wearing shorts. Really tight little ones that made his arse look like two snooker balls (there you go, you prick. I'm the one writing the book. Now who's wearing the shorts?).

We met there because the milkman always stopped on the corner of Herbert Avenue and delivered down the side roads before carrying on down Beaufort Road. He picked up a crate and carried it with him. Saved stopping and starting.

From memory his name was George. I think most milkmen are called George. Even the birds.

We hid behind the wall on the corner and watched him trundle down the road.

He stopped, as always (this is the key to most crime. Predictable and scheduled behaviour on the part of the victim.

If you don't want to be taken advantage of, live a less structured life. Best advice I can give you. Are you a security guard in a bank? Start doing your rounds randomly. Start showing up at work at weird times. Nobody will touch you).

He got out, picked up a crate of red-tops, put a couple of golds in there and one chocolate (because at least one mother on that street cared about her kids) and started walking away, not before turning off the motor.

Grey pulled his copy of Milkman's Weekly from his back pocket. He found it a few weeks ago chucked away at the side of the pavement. Right there, next to a white dog shit (don't see them anymore, do you? What happened to dogs? Why'd they start shitting different? That's a question for another day).

He held it up. Picture on the front was of a milk float. Same as the one that George had just left unattended.

Inside was the golden knowledge. That one thing the budding criminal needs. Secret information.

The magazine was very impressed with the new floats and was showing off all its wonderful advantages to a captive audience of jobbing milkman. Like where the red switch was located for starting and stopping the motor. It didn't have a fucking key. Can you believe it? We couldn't.

We started looking through the magazine for a laugh. Took the piss out of the pictures of milkman in their shorts. Fucking hate shorts, I do. Why do people want to display their knees?

We climbed over the wall, keeping low and keeping the milk float between us and George.

We watched him get right to the end of the road and then

we did it.

We stole the milk float.

Grey got in the driver's seat, and I lifted the double-wide seat next to it. The battery was kept under there and on top of it: the red switch. I flicked it and the motor whirred into life.

'Oi, you two, stop that,' he shouted, or something equally lazy and unimaginative. Like I said, it was a long time ago and I wasn't keeping notes.

George chased us. I threw milk bottles at him. You could call it a sport. I think it should be. He ran out of puff and stopped chasing about half a mile down the road.

We drove around for a while and then went down to Iford river to see how well these things really floated. Not very well, is the unsurprising answer.

Extract from *The Threat of Violence* by Pat Caine. Published by Underhand Books, 2013.

Pages 23 – 27

1974. The government were enforcing laziness by introducing a three-day-week. Can't remember the reason why exactly. I think the Conservatives had pissed off the miners and so the country had run out of power.

It was a Tuesday, approximately. One in seven chance it was, anyway. I was broke and living on Grey's couch.

We were in his flat. Grey was watching *Bagpuss* in his shorts. We were twenty-four. The TV was so old the side panel had to be fixed on with Blu Tack to stop it falling off every time the gongs went off during the news.

The power went out. Just like that. CLUNK. Bagpuss is there, and then he's not.

We lit some candles. It was very romantic.

Grey took whatever beer was left in the fridge. 'Might as well drink it, it will only go warm if we don't.'

He was right, so that's what we did.

Truth is, we were pretty much miserable. We didn't think it would be like this. We thought we'd be living it up by now, with the lights on and everything.

The country felt like it was running on empty, and we felt the same. The rich were safe and happy, and the working class was kicked in the dirt and left there to fend for ourselves. But we hadn't been fending for ourselves. We had been waiting for them to sort it out, and it didn't seem like they were going to any time soon.

I smoked back then. Packed it in the first time I got locked up. Good currency behind bars, if you can hold off smoking them. I gave one to Grey and we lit them on the candles.

I looked out the window. Grey's flat was above an off-licence, and it overlooked the NatWest bank on the high street across the road. The lights were off, and the staff left the bank early and locked up. The bank was already closed. It was after five, but the staff normally stuck around an hour doing whatever they do to close up shop.

'We should rob the bank,' I said.

Grey looked out the window. Thought about it. Shrugged. 'Alright.'

And that was that. The beginning of our illustrious career.

We tried to be clever the first time we did it. Spent ages scoping the place out. Kept making small withdrawals and deposits. The same money going in and out, so we had an excuse to go in and get a proper look around. Finesse our plans.

So many nights we sat at his coffee table drawing and redrawing a map to scale by memory. It was insanity. We were in love with the idea of doing it but couldn't bring ourselves to actually do it.

We had worked out that every Tuesday the manager was off. His wife went to the local Women's Institute to complain about shit, and he had to stay home and look after the baby.

That meant that Carl, the assistant manager, was responsible for locking up the bank, and he was not very responsible at all.

Week before we did the job, we got in touch with a guy named Pearson. He's dead now, so he won't mind me using his name. He managed to get a six-shooter for me, and three bullets. Cost fifty-three quid which—trust me—was a shit load of money back then.

Tuesday came around. We had set the date and stuck to it. We dressed in our normal clothes but put a pair of women's tights over our heads. Thought that was a pretty excellent disguise.

We watched from Grey's flat. Got to about five-forty in the evening. It was winter and already dark. All the staff had left. Carl was the only person in the bank. One thing Carl didn't do that the responsible manager did, was lock the door after the staff had left.

I don't know what they did in there, but the manager, or Carl, always came out fifteen minutes after the rest. I think somebody just had to be in there until six but there was no reason to keep the staff in. It was probably just in his job description. You can't leave the bank until six, so that's what they do. Jobsworths. The manager locked the door for those fifteen minutes. Carl did not.

On this Tuesday he had let the staff out five minutes early which gave us a twenty-minute window. Perfect.

So, there we were. Walked across the road with our tights on our heads and me with my gun in my pocket. Went straight up to the bank and let ourselves in.

There was no power cut on this Tuesday. All the lights were on.

Carl was sitting on the counter reading a newspaper.

I remember he looked up at us, saw that we were obviously there to rob him—I was, after all, pointing a gun at him—and he said, 'Sorry, we're closed.' Probably wasn't thinking straight.

Anyway, long story short. We made him open the safe and got out of there with twenty-three grand. And trust me, that really was a fuckload of money in those days. You could buy two houses with that.

We didn't get the chance. Police turned up the following morning. Carl described us. 'Thin white guy in an old suit. Big black guy in shorts (sorry Grey. He wasn't really wearing shorts... they were more like hot pants). Looked like the guys from across the road who come in all the time putting a fiver in and taking it out again. Thought there was something suspicious about those two.'

They tried to do us for armed robbery but couldn't find the gun (I had hidden it inside the fucked old TV set). We got put down for four years each as it was our first offence and we seemed desperate and like, 'A couple of decent lads who made a bad choice,' as the judge said.

They let us out after two for good behaviour. I made a lot of very useful contacts during those two years.

THANK YOU FOR READING

Now, scurry off and write an excellent review on Amazon.

If you enjoyed this and want to read more horror by me, check out **JACK'S GAME** on Amazon.

A coming-of-age horror for fans of *Stand by Me*, *IT*, and *Stranger Things* (if *Stranger Things* had an 18/R rating).

If you would like to sign up to my newsletter and hear about future releases before anyone else, you will find a sign-up page on my website — www.andychapwriter.com —You will also get a free short horror story when you sign up.

But, most importantly, as I said above, please leave a review. Even if it just says, 'Good.' The reviews trigger Amazon's algorithms into putting the book in front of more people. Us indie authors don't have the big marketing budgets, so your reviews are literally what keeps us going.

- Andy

ACKNOWLEDGEMENTS

It will be no surprise to anyone who knows me that Rachel Howells comes top of my list of people to thank. I would not be a writer without her. I returned to fiction to impress a girl. That's the truth. On the manic day of writing, Rachel stayed up with me. Filmed TikToks, Tweeted, encouraged, celebrated when I succeeded—she made it more than just a night at the desk.

I want to thank Julian Barr for his exceptional services as an editor. Thank you for making me look smarter than I am.

To all the beta readers that made Julian's job easier with the first round of feedback. Ian Sainsbury, Laura Regan, Kate Baker, Tracey Montague, Jackie Harmon, and Paul Ardoin.

Thank you to Mark Stay and Mark Desvaux at *The Bestseller Experiment* podcast for inspiring the idea and being my cheerleaders both on and off air.

Everyone who rallied around me on social media and sent supportive messages and tweets. You kept me going when my brain was failing.

I want to thank Vin, for being the best Vin that ever Vinned. You are awesome and I love you.

Finally, I want to thank the inventor of coffee. I don't know who you are, but from all writers everywhere, thank you.

Printed in Great Britain
by Amazon